TOO LATE, MR. EARLY!

Longarm stepped over the low stone wall and walked near to where the man was lying. He kicked the shotgun a little further away. He was amazed to see that the man with three heavy slugs in his chest was still breathing. Early said, "Wha . . . Who . . . are . . ."

Longarm said, "Does it really matter, Early, who I am? You're going fast, so I reckon you don't need to know all that bad. You just made a bad mistake. You should have shot me when you had the chance."

He hadn't finished speaking when Early closed his eyes and stopped breathing. Longarm jumped back across the wall to retrieve his rifle. He took a moment to reload the empty chambers of the spare gun he had been using. He stuck it back inside his waistband at the small of his back. It was a position that seemed to work fairly well.

TABOR EVANS

LONGARM

AND THE COLORADO COUNTERFEITER

JOVE BOOKS, NEW YORK

LONGARM AND THE COLORADO COUNTERFEITER

A Jove Book / published by arrangement with
the author

PRINTING HISTORY
Jove edition / January 1999

All rights reserved.
Copyright © 1999 by Jove Publications, Inc.
This book may not be reproduced in whole
or in part, by mimeograph or any other means,
without permission. For information address:
The Berkley Publishing Group, a member of Penguin Putnam Inc.,
375 Hudson Street, New York, New York 10014.

The Penguin Putnam Inc. World Wide Web site address is
http://www.penguinputnam.com

ISBN: 0-515-12437-0

A JOVE BOOK®
Jove Books are published by The Berkley Publishing Group,
a member of Penguin Putnam Inc.,
375 Hudson Street, New York, New York 10014.
JOVE and the "J" design are trademarks belonging to
Jove Publications, Inc.

PRINTED IN THE UNITED STATES OF AMERICA

10 9 8 7 6 5 4 3 2 1

LONGARM

AND THE COLORADO COUNTERFEITER

Chapter 1

Chief Marshal Billy Vail said, "Longarm, I'll tell you one thing. This is the damnedest situation I've ever run into in all my years behind the law." He was standing at the window of his office in the Federal Building in Denver, Colorado. He looked back over his shoulder at his deputy and said, "Custis, I still don't believe it." He turned back to the window and pointed. "But there is a man sitting in a fine home, a hundred miles from here on a mountain just outside of Silverton, Colorado, counterfeiting twenty-dollar bills, and nobody's been able to do a damned thing about it. What do you think about *that*?"

Custis said, "Well, Billy, I don't know what to think about that. It don't seem possible to me either. I mean, not in these modern times. I could see where in the old days they could make a fake greenback or one of the gold bank notes, but I just can't see where anybody would have the equipment or the ability or the skill to counterfeit any kind of bills, much less a twenty-dollar bill that is going to get a good looking at." He was seated in front of Billy Vail's desk with his boots up on a nearby chair. His full name was Custis Long and he was a deputy marshal in the Federal

Marshals' Service. He had worked for Billy Vail more years than either one of them cared to count. He had the wounds to show for it, but his face, weathered as it was, still could show the care and concern of a man dedicated to his duty.

Longarm was his nickname. It came from the fact that his last name was Long, and because there was no record of any criminal ever outrunning his reach. You could run and you could hide and you could sit on a mountaintop. You could dig a hole in the ground, you could go under the water. You could find a closet in a room in the biggest city you could think of, but sooner or later, Custis Long was going to show up with his "long arm of the law" and take you to justice. The nickname was used by his friends and enemies alike. It didn't bother him. He had never particularly cared for the name Custis anyhow. Sometimes, when Billy Vail was displeased, he could make the name Custis sound like the worst cuss word a man had ever heard.

Now, sitting there, Longarm was relaxed and smoking a cigarillo. He was a little over six foot tall and a little under two hundred pounds. His face said forty, but his body, which was hard with muscle, said thirty. His age didn't really matter. He had been a lawman long enough that his body and his brain knew what to do at the right times.

Billy Vail turned from the window and came and sat back down at his desk. Longarm was grateful. Billy wasn't very tall, but when he was standing up and Longarm was sitting down, the small chief marshal seemed to tower over him. Longarm didn't care to have his boss tower over him at any time, especially when he figured a very unpleasant assignment might be heading his way. Billy Vail said, "Yes, the man is counterfeiting twenty-dollar bills, as hard

2

as that is to believe. There's too much proof. There's been too many of them recovered. They're first-class work. I guarantee you, I could pass one off on you right now and you'd never be able to tell it.''

Longarm took his boots off the chair and dropped them to the floor with a clunk. He said, "Ha! Ha! I reckon that ain't so, Billy.''

Billy Vail looked up at him. "Oh, is that right? Have you by any chance got a hundred-dollar bill on you?''

Longarm gave him a slow look. "Yeah, I've got one on me. Just by chance, I do.''

"Where did you get it? Win it in a poker game? Or from shipping horses at government expense that you done brought back here to sell.''

Longarm said, "Now, don't start that old stuff again, Billy.''

"All right, I'll tell you what I'll do,'' Billy said. He reached in his back pocket and took out his wallet. From it, he took six twenty-dollar bills. "I'll give you these six twenties for that hundred. If there's anything wrong with any of them, I'll give you your hundred back if you can show me which one. You'll be ahead whichever twenty or forty or sixty dollars that you've got. How's that for a deal?''

Longarm sat up straight and reached in his pocket, saying, "Done. I guarantee you I can spot your bogus twenty-dollar bill. You give me to understand that you're going to give me six twenties and I'm going to give you a hundred. If any of them are counterfeit, I get to keep the rest of the twenties and I get my hundred back. Is that correct?''

Billy Vail nodded. "That's right.''

"Hand them over.''

Longarm took the six twenty-dollar bills, handing his

3

hundred to his boss, and then sat back down in the chair. One by one, he looked the bills over. Some of them were worn, some of them were fairly new, but they all looked genuine to him. After a moment, he put the bills together neatly, folded them, and then stuffed them into his pocket. "Billy," he said, "I just made twenty bucks off of you. That may well be the first time I ever got in your pocket."

Billy Vail looked at Longarm and chuckled quietly. He ran his hand through his thin graying hair. "So, you figure that you've got the best of it, do you? You figure that you're money ahead? Is that a fact?"

Longarm nodded. "Now, I know that you're about to tell me that I made a mistake, that two or three of these bills are counterfeit, or maybe all of them are bogus, but I'm not going to believe you. A man don't make a mistake about as big a bill as a twenty. Twenty-dollar bills are too hard to come by. Most folks I know give them a damned good looking over once they get their hands on one. No, I'll stand still on what I have."

Billy Vail laughed out loud. He leaned back in his chair and threw his arms into the air. "Oh, boy! I've got you, Longarm. It couldn't have happened to a nicer fellow." He leaned forward. "Three of those bills are real and three are counterfeit. You just took a forty-dollar bath is what you just did, Longarm, and I'm just happy as hell to give you the news."

Longarm sat back comfortably and gave Billy Vail a satisfied look. He said, "Shame on you, Billy, though I have to say it's just about what I expected. You and I both know that all six of those bills are genuine. You just hate to admit that I didn't find one or two that looked peculiar to me so you could have had a big laugh at just how much I knew.

Now, isn't that the case of the matter? You'll feel better for it."

Billy Vail chuckled again. "Longarm, I got those bills from a Treasury agent that was here at the bank. He made a dot of ink in the bottom right-hand corner of three of those bills. Get them out and you'll see what I'm talking about. Those three are bogus. Not worth the paper they are printed on. And by the way, it is a hell of a grade of paper, though not as good as what Uncle Sam uses."

Longarm gave his boss a skeptical look. "Billy, you are trying to put one over on me and I'm not going to stand for it."

"Go on, get those bills out. Hold them up to the light and take a look at them."

Still suspicious, Longarm took the six twenties out of his pocket. He had no trouble locating the three that had the small ink dot in the lower right-hand corner. But they didn't look or feel any different than the other three. He looked up, half smiling. "Billy, that ain't going to work. All these bills are good ones."

"Hold them up to the light."

Reluctantly, Longarm took one of the so-called bogus bills and one of the supposedly real ones and held them both up toward the window, looking at them. Billy Vail said, "Look real close. You can see small lines running through the real ones. That's the thread that's in the paper that the United States Government makes money out of. It's got cloth in it. Those counterfeit ones don't. They're straight paper."

Longarm glanced first at one bill and then at the other, adjusting them so that each had more light passing through. Very dimly, he could see the small veins of threads that Billy Vail was talking about in one bill. He laid it in his lap and took up another one that was supposedly good. Again, he could see the threads. He examined the third supposedly good bill, and then the other two that had the telltale dots in the corner. There were no threads in them, or in the first ink-dotted bill.

Longarm said, "I'll be damned, Billy. You sonofabitch, you just snookered me out of forty bucks. You ought to be ashamed of yourself. Taking a man's money who works as hard as I do."

Billy Vail shook with laughter, though none came out of his mouth. His eyes were dancing and he was busy slicking back his thin hair. "I knew you'd be too sure of yourself to pass up this good thing," he said. "Well, you just got taken, Longarm. I hope you enjoy it."

Longarm looked down at the money in his lap. "Well, that's fine and well that you took me, but I don't see how the average citizen out there on the street is going to be able to tell one of these bills from another. How did they find out in the first place? How did anybody know these were counterfeit?"

"Well, the Treasury Department, which operates a lot of banks, has a lighted piece of glass which they can run a bill over. In an instant, they can see if it's the right kind of paper. If they don't see what they are looking for, they know that something is wrong. That's the way they've gotten on to this fellow. They've traced him to where he is."

Longarm slowly put the money together, folded it again, and tucked it back into his pocket. "You mean to tell me that they know who is doing this?"

Billy Vail nodded his head. "That's a fact. They know his name, which is Ashton, and where he lives. He's got one hell of a spread up in the mountains on the other side of Silverton."

Longarm said, "What's his first name?"

"I think it's Vernon, but he gets called Vern. Anyway, he's run out about two million dollars. That's what the government figures. That's a hell of a piece of money that he's put over on United States citizens. I'm told that place of his looks like a palace and he has Hell's own men up there working for him. He's really got it set up."

Longarm said, "Well, why the hell don't they go in there and just shut him down? How come he's still operating?"

Billy Vail raised his eyebrows. "That, my friend, is where you come in."

A small frown passed across Longarm's face. He reached in his pocket and got out a cigarillo and a match, lit the match and then the cigarillo, and slowly drew on it while he studied his boss's face. He said, "What the hell are you talking about, Billy? It comes down to me? This is a United States Treasury problem. If this man is supposed to have run off two million dollars of those bills, they've got themselves a pretty good case. One lonesome deputy marshal ain't about to go in there and upset his apple cart anywhere near as good as the Treasury Department and the army and a half-dozen calvary detachments."

Billy Vail shook his head. "No, it can't be done that way. Now, listen. I'm telling you, this thing has been got at from every way there is to get at it. They've figured it from every angle. Let me tell you, the Treasury Department has been on to this fellow Ashton for a good while. But he's slicker than goose-grease. He ain't going to be taken easy."

"Why don't they just crash in there and shut him down?"

Billy Vail shook his head slowly and looked at Longarm as if he was ignorant. "Custis, don't you ever listen? By the time they got to getting at him, he would have hid his moneymaking machinery and all his paper stock and everything else somewhere back in those mountains where they could never be traced. He's got thirty or forty or fifty hired hands in that place. There ain't but one way to get at it, and that's straight up a canyon. There's going to be one hell of a fight before they can get to the castle this man lives in. By that time, there ain't going to be any evidence.''

Longarm lifted his hat and scratched his head. ''Well, how does the sonofabitch get it out of there?''

''That part ain't hard.'' Billy Vail shrugged. ''A pack mule, a wagon, you can haul a whole lot of twenty-dollar bills.''

''And he's just passing these things right and left?''

''All over the country. They've found them in Ohio, they've found them in Pennsylvania. They get passed around. He's in a nice location and he's hard to get at.''

Longarm said, ''What I don't understand is how this gent can make counterfeit money so good.''

''Well, that's the question that the Treasury Department wants the answer to. They don't know who made the plates that these bills are printed on. Somebody must really know how to do the engraving on those plates. If they had the paper stock from the United States Government, you couldn't tell his from ours.''

Longarm leaned over slightly. ''You said this was going to be up to me. You are not sitting there telling me that you expect me to go up to some hideout with forty or fifty hired *pistoleros* and bring back the bad man and all his boodle. You're not saying that, Billy, are you?''

Billy Vail chuckled. ''Sounds a good deal to me like *you're* saying it.''

''Well, that's just plain damned foolishness,'' Longarm

said with a little annoyance in his voice. "How in the hell do you expect me to get past all those guns? How do you expect me to get to this Vernon Ashton when a detachment of calvary can't even do it. That's silly, Billy. That's just damned foolish."

Billy Vail looked at him with his dry eyes and said coolly, "Custis, when you hired on with us, the idea was that you were supposed to do what you're told. Have you heard about anything changing since then?"

Longarm stared back for a moment. "No, you old son-ofabitch, you know damned good and well nothing's changed. But you're giving me a damned near impossible job."

"They gave it to me, and if I didn't have you to give it to, *I'd* have to do it. But I'm the chief marshal here, so that gives me the right to say that *you* have to go do it."

"How?"

Billy Vail shook his head again. "I don't know how. If I knew how, I could take any one of the new hands and send him up there to do it. You're the most experienced. You've got the best record and you keep telling me that you're the best deputy marshal that I've got. If you were me, wouldn't you give yourself the job?"

Longarm sighed. "You slick-talking sonofabitch. I'm just glad I ain't a woman. You'd have your hand in my britches before I knew what had happened."

"There ain't any chance of anybody taking you for a good-looking woman. They wouldn't mistake you for anything but what you are, which right now is somebody occupying my office when they ought to be out of here."

Longarm said, "I didn't think I'd have to leave out until the morning."

"That'll be soon enough. I think you need some time to spend planning and packing."

Longarm stood up. "I'm just supposed to head out of here with an extra horse and a pack mule, go over to Silverton, and hunt down this—what did you say his name was? Vernon Ashton? Slip up on him, do a job that a detachment of calvary can't do, and bring you back his head and those things you called engraving plates? Is that about the size of it?"

Billy Vail said, "You need to bring back the paper stock too. You might need to bring back any samples he has hanging around. And don't let any of them stick to your hands either."

"Oh, yeah. I understand now, Billy. So that's all there is to this job? I'm just supposed to sail on out of here like I know what I am doing?"

Billy gave him a dry look. "There will be a Treasury man coming around to your boardinghorse tonight about eight o'clock. He'll tell you everything you need to know."

"If he's so damned full of information, how come he doesn't go on and do it himself?"

Billy Vail threw his hands up. "Will you get the hell out of here and quit bothering me. Go and do your work so you won't have to back up to the pay window and get your money. For once, do an honest day's work."

Longarm shook his head as he came to his feet. "Boy, I'm glad I've got you for a boss, Billy. It's damned near better than being married. This way I get all the heartaches and headaches and I don't have to keep a wife up. I haven't had to buy you a new dress in quite a while."

He ducked as Billy Vail threw a small book at him, and then he turned for the door. "I reckon you know, Billy, that this sort of foolishness can get a man killed.''

Billy Vail said, "Get out of here!''

Longarm lay on his bed, thinking. His mind was awhirl
with details and plans and thoughts. He was in his room at
the boardinghouse, and the lady who owned a dress shop
who he considered his best girl was lying next to him. They
had just finished making love. It had not been very satis-
factory, mainly because Longarm couldn't get his mind off
the job. If anything, he was amazed that the Treasury Department, Billy Vail, or the President of the United States
for that matter, thought that he could go and do a job of
this size without any help. They weren't even offering another hired hand to hold his horse.

Almost idly, he reached over and ran his hand down her
smooth belly and into the furry patch where his girlfriend's
legs met. She was about thirty, but she was well kept for
her age. Pauline Gill was all lady in public, and all siren
once you got her in bed. She was about as fine a woman
as Longarm knew, and if he had been the marrying kind,
she would have been the one he chose. But for now, he
was content to stroke the silken patch of pubic hair and
then bring his hands up to feel her firm, erect breasts. As
he worked at it gently, the nipple of her right breast hard-
ened and stood out. He could feel her start to breathe heavier. It didn't take much to get her aroused, but he wasn't
sure he was up to it again.

Showing what he considered good sense, he stopped
fooling around with her body and put his mind back to the
visit earlier from the Treasury Department agent. Before
his thinking could run very far, Pauline said, "Don't you
want to?''

Longarm turned and looked at her. She had a sweet open

11

face and nice light brown hair. She had smooth, milky-tan skin. There wasn't much about her that he didn't like. "No, sweetheart, not right this minute. I've got something on my mind that's interfering with the lower part of me. Until I get this figured out, I'm not going to be much better than I was just now."

Pauline patted him on the thigh. "Now, don't you start worrying about that, honey. I didn't notice that it was any the less for your worries. Of course, your worst is generally better than most men's worst."

He gave her a mock severe look. "How would you know that? You told me that you were a virgin and that I was your first man."

Her eyes crinkled. "Oh, you are. I'm just telling you what I hear the ladies that come in my shop talk about."

Longarm half smiled. "They come in the door, do they, and talk about making love?"

"Of course."

He let out a low whistle. "I reckon I've been hanging around the wrong places. I need to stay out of saloons and hang around your dress shop."

She gave his thigh a little slap. "Never you mind about any other ladies. When you are in Denver, you're mine."

"Well, right now, I've got to do some thinking. Why don't you go on to your room. I'll come down later and we'll have another go at this thing."

"All right." With a smooth move, she was off the bed and gathering up her dress. Longarm enjoyed watching her lithe shapely body as she pulled her legs into her undergarments and then shrugged the bodice over her shoulder. She was a handsome woman indeed. In a moment, she was dressed. She didn't bother with her stockings or her shoes, but simply went to the door and blew him a kiss. She said, "Come down when you can."

From the bed, he nodded, "All right, honey. I've got to do a little thinking."

She disappeared. He had not told her that he would be leaving the next morning for a long job. He thought it might have intefered with the pleasure of his last night in town. But as it turned out, the Treasury agent had been the one who had intefered with his last night in town.

Chapter 2

The Treasury agent's name was Ladell Sump. He was a young man, younger than Longarm. The deputy marshal guessed the agent to be in his early to mid-thirties. He was very businesslike, very sure of himself, and very confident. At the time, Longarm thought that he was very free and easy with Longarm's time and trouble.

Sump had come up to his room a little after eight o'clock. Together they sat down across a small square table. Sump laid out in as much detail as he could all that he knew about Vernon Ashton and his affairs and how the man operated.

He began by saying, "You understand, Marshal. . . ."

"I'm a deputy marshal."

"All right, Deputy. You understand that counterfeiting has been around for a long time?"

"Yes, I understand that, Mr. Sump, but let's just stick to this one counterfeiter in particular since this is the only one I ever expect to be after."

"The advantage that he has had over any others that we have ever run across is the quality of his paper. We think that he might have been in the papermaking trade somewhere or another. We have canvassed the country and all the appropriate companies, trying to find a very experienced employee who might have left in the past couple of years. I say the last couple of years, because that's how long we think this man has been operating.''

Longarm said, ''Go on.''

''So far, we haven't come up with anything. We've found several men who have retired, but they didn't pan out. Either they were not experienced in making this grade of paper, or we were able to locate them and determine that they could not be this man who we call, and who calls himself, Vernon Ashton. We think the actual counterfeit plates that the bills are printed on were engraved in Germany. We have no sure knowledge of that, but that has been where the best engraving has been done. It could be that we're all wrong. It could be that this man is an engraver and he's getting his paper stock from another source. It's hard to tell. It is so damned close to United States Government stock that we at first suspected that our own supplier was selling him some of the seconds or thirds of the paper that didn't quite fit our grade. But every sheet has to be accounted for, and every one of them *were* accounted for, so you can see where we are.''

Longarm said, ''I can see where I am. You want me to go charging up a canyon with about thirty or forty hired hands shooting at me while this guy buries all the swag and I get shot dead.''

Sump cleared his throat. ''I was given to understand from your immediate supervisor, Chief Marshal Billy Vail, that you are a man of some mental resources and that you would find a way to infiltrate this operation and to get close to Mr. Ashton and the counterfeit goods before he could hide them or destroy the evidence.''

Longarm grimaced. "A few more compliments like that and I can go to making arrangements with the undertaker. No, Mr. Sump, I don't have that kind of mental resources, whatever that means, and I damned sure don't have any idea how I'd infiltrate this man's operation, whatever infiltrate means. All I know is that I've been given a job that I think should be yours. What do you think of that?"

Sump didn't have the good grace to look uncomfortable. "Well, that's not the way it worked out, Deputy Long. We asked for the Marshals Service to assist us in this matter. We were given permission to use any and all of their resources. Your chief marshal said you were the best resource he had. So, it's your job."

"I suppose I just can't up and say I won't do it."

Sump nodded slowly. He was not a man who seemed to smile very much. He said, "Yes, you can do that, Marshal. I would imagine that it would result in your immediate dismissal."

"Is that the same thing as being fired?"

"It's the same thing as being fired without any hope of getting your pension."

Longarm gave him a look. He quickly decided he didn't like this man. He said, "If I go up into this canyon, I don't think a pension is going to do me any good at all."

Sump was wearing a bowler hat. He took it off, wiped his forehead on his arm, and then put the severe black creation back on his head. "That's entirely up to you, Marshal. . . or Deputy. Excuse me. My job is to tell you everything I know." He stood up. "I have done that. Now, let's see what results you can get."

Longarm said to Pauline, "Sump. S-U-M-P. Ladell Sump. Can you imagine a man walking around with such a name?'' He cocked his head at her. "I mean, I don't like the sonofabitch anyway, but I sure don't like him with a name like that. Coming in here, telling me what I got to do and how I've got to do it, and all that.''

He was sitting on the bed, dressed. She was sitting in the chair across from him looking very trim in a light cotton frock. It made his mouth water as he looked at her breasts straining at the thin material of her bodice. She said, "Custis, I don't quite understand just what your job is this time. You didn't exactly tell me about it, so I have no way of knowing.''

He shrugged. "Aw, honey, there ain't no point in talking about it. It's just another damned job. They all start to run together after a while. Go here, do that. Fetch this man, fetch that one. Catch this one, catch that one. Doesn't matter whether he's stolen a horse or robbed a bank or what he's done—the job still pays the same. Are you going to miss me while I'm gone?''

She looked down and fluttered her eyelashes. "That depends on how long you're going to be gone.''

Longarm shrugged. "I don't know. All I know is that I'm not looking forward to being gone from here and gone from you.''

She said, "Well, how long do you think it will be? A week? Two days? A month?''

Longarm shrugged again. "I don't know. I would guess however long it takes to do the job. Maybe I can get it done in a week. If I can, that's what I'm going to do. How come you're asking that? Is there a certain amount of time that I'd better not be gone beyond? Are you going to take up with another fellow if I'm gone longer than, say, two weeks?''

She gave him the faintest of smiles. "I didn't say that.''

Longarm laughed. "No, but you damned well hinted at it, you little vixen."

She said, "I just wanted to give you a reason to hurry back as quick as you can."

He winked at her. "You already did. Earlier this morning."

It was not long until noon. She had come into his room that morning, and they had made love. Now, she was dressed to go to her shop and he was dressed to go on the train. Pauline had taken time off to be with him during these last few hours of the morning, and he had been grateful. He said, "Well, honey, I'm going to get back just as fast as I can."

"Just make sure it's in one piece."

"I sure hope to hell it is," he said. "But as much as I know about this job, I can't guarantee anything. Now, why don't you give me a quick kiss and run along to your dressmaking business. I've got a bunch of stuff to do before I get on that damned train. I've got two horses to load and some other errands to run."

He stood up and walked toward her. She rose as he did, and he gave her a lingering kiss on the mouth. After that, he watched her as she walked out the door. He shrugged as it closed, and said under his breath, "Damn you, Billy Vail. And damn you, Ladell Sump. Ladell Sump. What a name."

Longarm left his boardinghouse with his saddlebags over his shoulders and carrying a small valise. His saddlebags contained an extra .44–.40 revolver, the handgun of his choice. It was a .40-caliber Colt on a .44-caliber frame. The .40-caliber was strong enough to stop a man, but the .44 frame was heavier and sturdier in the hand and caused less

19

barrel deviation. His rifle was in his saddle boot at the livery stable, where the two horses he intended to take with him were being kept. In the valise were two changes of clothes and a blanket, just in case he had to sleep out. He had packed his saddlebags with some jerked beef, cheese, crackers, and canned goods he had bought at a store near his boardinghouse. Longarm's landlady had given him a good breakfast, and he had had a good lunch at a cafe nearby. He walked to the livery stable and took out his two horses. One was a big, strong bay gelding that was fast and had a little staying power. Longarm was also taking a small dapple-gray mare that he knew to be calm and confident under gunfire and that could keep a trail for twenty-four hours if need be, if she wasn't pushed too hard. The gelding was a four-year-old. The mare was pushing eight. He had the stable boy bring them out and follow him as he walked to the depot.

He still had not the slightest idea how he was going to get close to Mr. Vernon Ashton, or even how he was going to ask him to quit making counterfeit twenty-dollar bills. First, Longarm had to get in the general vicinity of where the man lived. Then he would have to see what the ground looked like, what the situation looked like, and plan from there. He had never been much of a hand for planning a campaign a hundred miles away from the site of the action.

Longarm had ordered a stock car the night before, and now he loaded his horses into the slatted car that came complete with feed and hay and water. He made himself a seat on a bale of hay, and put his saddle and his rifle and his other gear down close to hand. The horses, as always, had been nervous walking up the ramp and into the unusual confines of a stock car. But soon enough, they were busy with the feed and the water, and had quit looking around in amazement at finding themselves in such a place. Long-arm gave the stable boy a half dollar for his help, and then pulled the sliding car door shut. There was still a good half hour until train time, but he figured he'd make do with his time. He had brought along four quarts of his special Maryland whiskey, and he figured that some of that would do him to drink.

Before the train started off, he spent some time inspecting his weapons, making sure that they were in working order. Both of his handguns had just been cleaned. One was a rimfire, double-action Colt with a six-inch barrel that he used for close-in work. The other was a single-action, the mate to the first pistol, except it had a nine-inch barrel. He didn't use it often, but whenever he needed something between a handgun and a rifle, it was a mighty convenient weapon. The rifle held six rounds, the same as the handguns. Both the handguns had floating firing pins, so there was no necessity of keeping an empty cylinder under the hammer. He had one last weapon. His belt buckle was big and concave and inside it was a .38-caliber derringer, held in place with a steel spring. More than once, it had been his final resort and it had saved his life.

Longarm sat back, not thinking much of anything, just waiting. Finally, the train started with a jerk and a flurry of smoke and steam and the clanking of cars. Little by little, it began to pull away from the station in Denver. He looked through the slats at the size of the city. He was always amazed at how it was growing. All around were mountain peaks and valleys. It was rough, hard country, and it took rough, hard men to handle it. He wondered if he would be rough and hard enough to handle a man who was doing something Longarm hadn't even known could be done.

The horses had seemed to take the train's start well

enough, though they had spooked and jumped around a little bit. Now that the going was easier, they had settled down, and were eating grain and were looking perfectly content to take a train ride. Silverton was only a hundred miles away, straight across the peaks and valleys, but it took considerably longer by way of the railroad, which had to wind around the mountains and the chasms and the deep valleys. Normally, it was about a six- or seven-hour trip. Longarm hoped he would get in earlier. It was late July, and it usually got dark about 7:30. He was hoping to get to the area in time to maybe have a chance to ride out and have a look at what he was up against. But with the pace of the train being what it was, he figured he'd be spending the night in a hotel room in Silverton. Maybe, if he was lucky, he could find a poker game. And maybe, if he was really lucky, he'd find some talkative strangers who could tell him a little something about this Vernon Ashton.

He thoughtfully pulled one of the bottles of Maryland whiskey out of one of his saddlebags, uncorked it, had a good pull, and then shoved the cork back home again and replaced the bottle. It was the kind of whiskey that was smooth enough that you didn't need to chase it with water to put out the fire. He'd always been partial to it, but he couldn't always get it, so he always tried to take as much of it with him as he could. He remembered a time in Colorado when a desperado had jumped him in his hotel room. The man had come in firing. He had missed Longarm with his first four shots, but he had busted the three quarts of good whiskey that were sitting on the bedside table. Longarm had almost had tears in his eyes as he'd finally shot the man in the chest, knocking him out in the hallway. If he'd had his way, he would have rather had the man take an ear off him, or maybe wound him slightly in the shoulder, than break that much whiskey. But that was life in the Marshals Service, and there wasn't a damned thing he could do about it.

The train rocked along. After a time, Longarm went over to the door of the car and slid it back so he could see out. Sometimes, the train would run alongside a gorge or a deep valley, and he could see down a thousand feet to the rocks and the grass and the trees below. He kept a good grip on the slats of the car. Just the sight of that much empty air made him about half dizzy. It was a long ride, and he was anxious to get there and get on the ground to see what he could find out. Finally, Longarm sat down and made another meal out of the biscuits, the jerky, and the cheese. The horses looked contented enough. But then, what the hell did they know? They didn't have to figure out how to get up a canyon and make their way into a house where a man was making twenty-dollar bills illegally.

He dozed off and on, and then, after what seemed like an eternity, he could feel the train slowing, and he knew the next station was Silverton. He got up, got his horses rigged, and put his saddle on the gray mare and the saddlebags on the four-year-old gelding. When they came skidding to a halt, there were a couple of railroad roustabouts that brought a ramp up to his car and shoved it into place. One at a time, Longarm led his horses out of the stock car. They didn't like stepping on the springy boards of the ramp, but they came along well enough.

After that, he cinched up the saddle on the mare and then transferred his saddlebags behind him. His valise he tied to the saddle horn of the big saddle. Then he walked into the train depot, looking for the passenger agent. He found him behind his grilled cage, a small, stooped man wearing a green eyeshade. Longarm asked him where the best accommodations in town were.

The man glanced up and gave Longarm a measured look. "Well, stranger," he said, "there's three, so you can take your pick. There is Mrs. Bender, who runs a boardinghouse right at the edge of town. Can't miss it. Got a big sign out in front. She has clean beds and she sets a pretty fair table. Then the Nugget Saloon has got rooms upstairs. They'll cost you a little more because you'll be that much closer to the gambling. Then there's the Silverton Hotel. It's kind of run-down, but it's still pretty fair. As good as you'll find in this part of the country."

Longarm thanked the man, and then stepped aboard the gray and started toward the town. He elected for the Silverton Hotel because he knew they would have a livery stable and he wanted his horses close at hand and he wanted them seen to properly.

The hotel was about a half mile away. The bay gelding he led right alongside his right leg as they jogged toward the center of the town. He reckoned it to be one of those places with somewhere around a thousand in population—two thousand when times were good, five hundred when times were bad. At one time, it had been a boomtown in silver, and he could see from the deserted buildings that the town had once been two or three times its present size. Now, it had settled down to just a steady run of silver, and a set number of miners were kept employed in the one mine that was left.

It was late evening, and the air was still warm and light. He could feel the altitude. Silverton was higher than Denver. Longarm figured it was about 6500 feet, and was set atop a high grassy plain that was ringed with mountains on all sides but the south.

As he pulled up in front of the hotel, Longarm noticed that the streets were mainly deserted. He figured that was because it was close to the supper hour. He reckoned most people with any sense would have their feet under the dinner table. He stepped down from the mare, dropping the reins to the ground, and walked into the hotel.

The man at the desk looked up. Longarm said, "I want a ground-floor room for a few days. I've got two horses out front and I want them seen to."

The clerk said, "That will be two dollars a day in advance for you and a dollar apiece for the horses. Four dollars per day."

Longarm could have pulled out his badge, and there wouldn't have been any talk about advance payment, but he had decided that he would just lay low on this particular trip and wait until it had become absolutely necessary to declare himself a lawman. He dug down in his pocket, pulled out a double eagle, and flipped it on the counter. He said, "Use that until it's gone, and then let me know when you need more."

The clerk nodded. "Yes, sir. I'll get a boy out to see to your horses right away. Your room is number three, just down that front hall. You've got a view of the street."

Longarm picked up his valise, nodded at the clerk, and started down toward his room.

After he had eaten dinner at the hotel dining room, he wandered down to the Nugget, the biggest saloon in town. They had faro, they had roulette, and there were a number of individual poker games going on. Poker was one of Longarm's favorite passions, as were Maryland whiskey and fine women, and he prided himself that he had reduced the game to one of skill more than luck. Billy Vail never failed to go off into the gales of laughter when Longarm said such things. But then, Billy Vail never noticed how much he was losing while he was laughing.

Longarm selected a chair at a game with five other players. They seemed to be anteing a half dollar and playing pot limit. It was the kind of game he liked, the kind where you could protect your hand with a big bet and keep someone from drawing out on you.

He nodded as he sat down. "Howdy, gents. Any rules?"

One of the men said, "Play what you have in front of you. Check and raise. Other than that, play your best five cards."

Longarm carefully counted out seventy-five dollars. He anted for the first hand. The cards came around in a game of stud, one down and four up, with a bet after each card. He caught a king in the hole with the first card, and then a king up on his second card. He bet two dollars.

The man who had given him the rules gave him a brief smile, and said, "Kings wired, neighbor?"

Longarm smiled back with the same amount of humor. "Always. What good is one king without another unless it's in a straight or a flush? How about that queen you've got showing? Got another little lady in the hole?"

The man said, "Sure enough. Like you say, what good is one without another?"

The hand went on, with the bets going up as the cards went around. Soon, the man with the queen and Longarm were the only two left in the game. The man with the queen had caught a pair of deuces besides the queen. If he had a queen in the hole, he'd have two pair. He bet twenty-five dollars into Longarm. Longarm was still holding only a pair of kings. He was holding a seven and an eight besides. After a long study, knowing that he was trusting luck and

26

that this seemed as good a time as any to test it, he called the bet. Then he was dealt his fifth card. It was a seven. Then the man with the queen and the pair of deuces. It was a king. The man smiled at Longarm. He said, "Looks like I caught your king, neighbor. That kind of cuts down on the odds of you having one in the hole, don't it?"

Longarm said, "You could say that." The only danger now was if the man had a deuce in the hole, giving him three deuces. If he had that, he had the winning hand. If not, Longarm had the best of the two pair with a pair of kings over sevens against a pair of queens over a pair of deuces. His sevens were high, and he cautiously bet ten dollars. The man raised him back twenty.

Now Longarm had to study. It was a healthy raise, unless the man was holding a third deuce. He looked up at the man, trying to see the size of the pupils in the man's eyes. Sometimes you could tell how excited a man was by the pupils. They drew up and got small when a man was scared. This man's pupils seemed just an ordinary size. Longarm thought a moment, then called the raise and raised twenty back. Now the man stared at him. Longarm leaned forward in a comic way and opened his eyes. He said, "What do you reckon? They look about the same?"

The man suddenly laughed and turned his cards face-down. He said, "Hell, if you can't take a joke, forget it."

Longarm pulled in the pot. He said, "I would have bet a pretty that you were laying there playing cat-and-mouse with a third deuce in the hole."

"I wish I was. Did you have that pair of kings?"

Longarm gave him an innocent look. "Of course I had the pair of kings. You're not supposed to lie in poker, are you?"

The man smiled again. "No, no. Whoever heard of lying in poker?"

After about another hour or so, the game broke up as one player after another went bust. Longarm and his initial adversary were winning fairly steadily. Sometimes they went head up against each other in the big pots, but only when it couldn't be avoided. Longarm won his share, but the other man was also a skilled player. Finally, Longarm pushed his chair back and said, "I've had enough. I'm going to the bar and get a drink."

The man across from him stood up also and said, "That sounds like a damned good idea. Mind if I join you?"

Longarm said, "Hell, you're the big winner. I reckon you ought to buy."

The man gave a chuckle. "You can say I'm the big winner, but you saying it don't make it so. You and I both know who the big winner was."

Longarm laughed and slapped the man on the back as they walked toward the bar. He said, "Have it your own way then. One thing I won't ever deny is being the big winner. I don't play poker to lose, and when I do lose, I'm generally in a foul mood."

They each put a boot on the brass railing, and they called for a bottle of whiskey with two glasses. Longarm had been studying his acquaintance all evening. The man had never said his name, and Longarm had never said his. He took them to be of a close age. Longarm's face said forty, but his body said thirty. This man's face said forty, and his body also said forty. He was a little pudgy where Longarm was hard and slim. But he had a good-natured face and a glib tongue, and he wore a six-gun in a fashion that let you know he knew how to use it but that he wasn't in any particular rush. He had the hammer tied down with a leather thong. It was a way of saying, "I can use this thing if I have to, but if you draw on me before I have a chance to get this hammer free, then you are shooting an unarmed man."

Longarm thought it was a good sensible practice. After they had toasted to luck and drunk off half the whiskey, he gave his name to the man. He used his regular name, Custis Long, because he doubted that it would be known. It was his nickname by which he was usually recognized.

The man put out his hand and they shook. He said, "Finley is my name. Joe Finley. Are you from around here, Mr. Long?"

Longarm shook his head and said, "No, Mr. Finley. I just got into town today. I'm sort of looking around to get the lay of the ranching business in these parts."

Finley said, "That be so? Well, I kind of dabble in the cattle business myself. Might be I could tell you a little about the area, although I don't live here. I've got one place around here that I've been trying to improve so I could raise some cattle. At this high altitude, you can get some mighty fine grass into your livestock and raise some damned good beef. But it's hard to get that first crop of grass to come in. I've got a pretty good-sized pasture up north of here that I've been trying to get going. We've plowed it under three years running, and this might just be the year I let it come on and turn cattle in on it next year. It's going to be fall here pretty soon, and it'll be time to tuck it under if I'm going to do it."

Longarm studied the whiskey in his shot glass. It wasn't Maryland whiskey, but it wasn't all that bad. He said, "I've heard that there is a man around here that hires a goodly number of riders. Would you have any idea about him?"

Finley's eyes narrowed, and his good-humored face

seemed to crease and darken. He said, "Would you be talking about a man that don't seem to be in the cattle business
or the horse business or the goat business or the sheep
business, but yet he keeps about forty riders working for
him? All of them hardcases? Would that be the gentleman
you're talking about?"

Longarm said, "That could be. The name is Ashton. Vernon Ashton. It could be the gent I'm inquiring about."

Finley said, "Well, I can't help you in that direction."
He tossed down his whiskey, wiped his mouth with his
sleeve, and then flipped a five-dollar gold piece on the bar.
"Glad to have met you, Mr. Long, and good luck. It's
about time for me to turn in now."

Longarm took a half step after the man. "Hold up, Mr.
Finley. You seem to know a good bit about Mr. Ashton.
Maybe I'm walking into something I shouldn't be walking
into. Maybe you could warn me off of him."

Finley stopped and looked back at Longarm. There were
the sounds of the crowded saloon all around him, but his
words came through clear and distinct. "Yes," Finley said.
"You might be getting into something you might not ought
to, but then it's not for me to say what you ought to be
getting in to. Excuse the language, Mr. Long, but I don't
know a damned thing about you. You may be just what
Vernon Ashton is looking for."

Longarm said, "I'd like to talk to you some more, Mr.
Finley."

The man nodded and turned toward the door. "I'm staying at the hotel," he said. "I ain't hard to find."

Longarm turned back to his drink. In a way, he was
heartened. He had expected to find the whole town solidly
behind Vernon Ashton, mainly because the man was sup-
porting a big payroll, which could mean a lot of money in

a town the size of Silverton. But also, he had expected to be met with hostility. He doubted that Vernon Ashton cared much to have his business inquired into. Longarm finished his drink and set his glass back on the bar. After that, he pushed back, turned slowly, and headed toward the door, his mind working. At least now, he had a little something to work on.

Chapter 3

Longarm was up early, and hung around the lobby until he saw Joe Finley come down the stairs and head into the dining room. He waited a few moments for the man to be seated, and then walked into the room himself. A quick glance showed that the man was seated at a small corner table. Longarm ambled over and pulled a chair out. He looked down at Finley and said, ''Mind if I sit down, neighbor?''

Finley looked slightly surprised, but not displeased. He shrugged and said, ''Help yourself. They've got chairs for everybody. I believe this is what you call a common dining hall.''

Longarm sat down and pulled his chair up. Almost as soon as he was settled, a black waiter appeared at his elbow, poured him some coffee, and asked if he cared for cream. Longarm shook his head and said, ''No, no need to weaken it down with any cow's squeezings. Only thing I like in this coffee that ain't coffee is a little Maryland whiskey.''

Joe Finley looked up at Longarm, startled. He said, ''Don't tell me you're a Maryland whiskey man.''

Longarm nodded. "I'm a Maryland whiskey man enough that I brought four quarts with me on this trip. But you're the first man I've run into in some time that even knows what it is."

Finley laughed shortly. "Well, don't be letting the secret out. That would mean that much less for us. Hell, I've been drinking Maryland whiskey ever since I was old enough and had enough money to appreciate the better things in life."

Longarm said, "But where in the world did you run across Maryland whiskey? I take it that you're from this part of the country."

Finley shook his head slowly. "No. The reason I know about Maryland whiskey is that I'm originally from Maryland. I've been out here for about fifteen or twenty years, and I have a hell of a time keeping it in supply. You know, they don't make much of that stuff. It's pretty hard to get it shipped to you in quantities less than a box car-load."

Longarm got out a cigarillo and lit it and laughed slightly. "Well, a box car-load is quite a bit of whiskey, but maybe we could go in halves on one."

Finley laughed, and a good feeling settled in between them. It had been Longarm's intention to befriend the man. He felt that Finley was someone who might furnish some help.

The waiter came and took their orders and they ate. They both had ham and eggs and stewed tomatoes. It was a surprisingly good meal for that part of the country, and Longarm was grateful for the silent time as they ate. It gave him a chance to think about an approach to the subject he wanted to talk to the man about. Finally, after they had put their forks and knives down, wiped their mouths, and settled down with their last cups of coffee, Longarm said,

"Now, listen here, Mr. Finley. I may have given you the wrong impression last night. I don't know what those riders do that work for this man Ashton, but I got the impression from you that they generally are up to no good. What are they? A rough lot? A bunch of *pistoleros*?"

Finley shifted his eyes and looked carefully toward the tables nearest them. He cleared his throat and said in a lowered voice, "Mr. Long, it ain't real good politics to discuss, out loud Mr. Ashton or his men or what they do."

Longarm could feel the hair rise on the back of his neck. Did the whole town know that Ashton was in the counterfeiting business? He said noncommittally, "Is that so?"

Finley nodded his head. "Yes. Vernon Ashton and his operation are important to this town. They spend a lot of money here, and you're going to find that a lot of the folks are not interested in someone coming around and messing things up, if you take my meaning."

Longarm tried to look innocent. "Well, what are they doing? Are they doing something illegal?"

Finley shook his head. "I couldn't tell you that, Mr. Long. I don't know that much about Ashton or his men or what they do. Like I told you last night, he ain't got no sheepherders out there, he ain't got no cattlemen, and he ain't got nobody chasing billy goats. Now, what he needs with forty well-armed, well-mounted men is beyond me. He makes me nervous, but maybe that's just my own problem."

"Well, do they come into town and create a big wad of trouble?"

Finley shook his head. "No. As a matter of fact, it's just the opposite. Never more than six or seven or eight of them come in at one time, and they are just as polite as someone in your aunt Martha's parlor. No trouble, no fights. You couldn't ask for a better-behaved bunch of men. They're even young, most of them in their late twenties and early thirties. I'd say there's not a man of them, except for his foreman, who is approaching forty. They come in, drink their whiskey, have their time with the girls upstairs in the Nugget Saloon, buy what they need at the stores, and then they get on out of town before a fresh bunch comes in. They kind of rotate them, if you understand what I mean, so they don't stay out there on that ranch too long."

"So it's a ranch, is it?"

Finley looked up at him. "Well, I call it a ranch only because it's a bunch of grass. I don't call it a ranch because it's full of cattle. As far as I know, there is no cattle out there. Maybe they keep a few head for butchered meat, but on that amount of land, he could run a thousand head. He ain't got nowhere near that number on that beautiful highland's prairie. He's got plenty of good horses, though. Plenty. Several animals you might even call racehorses."

"And this Ashton just lives out there by himself?"

Finley shrugged again. "Mr. Long, you're going to have to ask someone who knows more than I do. I've been coming here for a good number of years." Finley stopped and thought a moment. "I guess Ashton got set up there about five or six years ago. I can't be sure of that. He just kind of grew from nothing. And I've never been on the place, I've never spoken to the man, but I have seen him from across the street. That's the best I can tell you."

Longarm said, "Doesn't that strike you as kind of funny, his hired hands being so polite and nice and all? I've never seen a bunch of riders when they came into town that didn't cause *some* kind of trouble. You say his bunch doesn't cause any?"

Finley took a sip of coffee. "I've never heard of them

causing any trouble. I find it passing strange myself, but then I don't live here, Mr. Long. You have to remember that. I've just got some property scattered around the area, and I come down here to look after it every now and again. Ashton is just a curiosity to me. But I will tell you this— these folks around this town are damned interested in keeping him happy and seeing that nobody interferes with his business. If I were you, I wouldn't go around asking a whole bunch of questions."

Longarm said, "Well, hell. What does a man do if he's got his curiosity up?"

Finley cast a thoughtful eye at Longarm. "If he's got any sense, he keeps his mouth shut where some areas are involved."

"Well, I can't see how a man can sit out there on a big patch of grass without any cattle and pay that many hired hands and stay afloat and keep his head above water. How does he make a living? Does he have a mine out there?"

"Mr. Long, I can't tell you any other way than I have already done, but I don't know any more about Mr. Ashton and his business than what I've told you. If you're that interested, why don't you ride out there and ask him for that job you say you want? I do have to tell you, I don't think you're going to get a job tending cattle if that's what you have in mind."

"I don't remember, Mr. Finley, telling you I was looking for a job."

"I sure got that impression last night."

"Well, it happens that ain't the case. It happens that I am in the horse-breeding business. I have heard that this Ashton fellow will pay top dollar for good horseflesh."

Finley scratched his chin. He hadn't shaved that morning, and it made a little *scritch-scratch* sound. He said,

"Then I guess I misunderstood you. I didn't get that impression off of you last night."

"I am in the horse business."

"Well then, I don't see why you don't just ride on out there and see what Mr. Ashton thinks of your stock. I assume that if you are trading stock, you have some with you."

Longarm had almost put himself into the trap. He did not have the quality of horseflesh with him that he was talking about, and he said, "No, not really. This was just a stop on my way west, where I am looking to pick up some orders from some cattle ranchers in Oregon and out toward there. I heard about this Ashton, and it made me curious. All I have with me is some ordinary riding stock. But I don't think it would hurt to go out and proposition Ashton, and see if he's interested in looking at some good blooded stock that I could bring his way."

Finley said, standing up, "Well, I wish you luck, Mr. Long. Me, I've got to get out there and look at my small plots of land. I ain't like Mr. Ashton. I don't own a big broad prairie right in the middle of a bunch of nice land. I've never seen a better place to finish off high-grade beef in all my life, and he's out there, running around, doing I don't know what."

Longarm stood up also and put two dollars on the table. "Does he keep a wife or a girlfriend?"

Finley shook his head again. "I don't know whether you keep a wife or a girlfriend, Mr. Long, and I don't know the same thing about Mr. Ashton. Good day to you, sir."

Longarm watched him walk away. His mind was working, trying to find a crack to lever himself onto the so-called ranch of Vernon Ashton. It was clear to him from what Finley had said that there wasn't much use hanging around

38

town asking questions, trying to get advance information on the doings out at Ashton's place. Longarm was going to have to saddle up and go have a look for himself.

Back in his room, he checked his firearms, including the derringer that fit in the conclave buckle of his gun belt. He made sure his revolvers were loaded and cleaned, as well as his Winchester carbine. It was just habit. There was very seldom a time when they weren't clean and fully loaded. But you didn't get as old as Longarm was by being careless.

He had the mare saddled and brought around. He put his extra six-gun into his saddlebags, filled his canteen, slung it off his saddle, rammed his rifle home in the boot, and then stepped aboard and set off. The clerk at the hotel desk had given him directions. He'd said, "Oh, it ain't hard to find, Mr. Long. You just go out south of town. Take that road that runs right through there. After about a mile, you'll see a small sign with nothing on it but an arrow nailed to a post that points off at about a forty-degree angle to the left. You can see it aimed toward the mountain peaks. Take it in that direction.

"There will be a sort of buggy road that you can follow. It ain't no proper road, it's just used enough that you can tell where it's going. Follow that. It's going to climb on you some because Mr. Ashton's place is about a thousand feet higher than where we are, so you'll be moving on up. Keep following that road and keep sighted in on those peaks.

"Pretty soon, you'll come to a close place between two mountainsides. You get in through there—plenty of room for your horses. It's narrow on account of the size of the Rocky Mountains on each side of you. Get on through that notch in the mountains, and then a great big, wide green-as-grass prairie will open up in front of you. It's bordered on each side by the peaks of that string of small mountains that runs this way off the Rockies. Now, after that, you just ride toward the end of that pasture. In there, you'll run into Mr. Ashton's house. You can't miss it. It's a big one. It's made out of rock and brick and some lumber. It's about the biggest house in this part of the country. But I imagine before you go very far, you'll have a guide.''

Longarm hadn't bothered to ask what he meant by that. He could guess. One of the forty or so riders that worked for Ashton would intercept him. The question was whether Longarm could talk the guide into taking him up to the house to meet Ashton. He supposed that it all depended on how good his line of bull was about being a horse trader, a horse breeder, and in the horse business in a big way. He didn't reckon he'd impress a man like Vernon Ashton just talking about ordinary hundred-dollar saddle ponies.

Now, in the bright sunshine of late morning, he passed down the main street of the town, and leaving it behind, putting the mare into a slow lope. He was following the mountain wagon road that he supposed went to a silver mine and then, maybe, on to the next town. Before long, Longarm saw the signpost sticking up like a scarecrow. It was blank, but it had an arrow pointing off to one direction, and he veered to his left and slowed to a pace suitable for the rough footing underneath.

Just as the clerk had told him, the ground began to climb. In some places, the incline was steep enough that the mare was huffing and blowing a little bit. From time to time, Longarm stopped to give her a chance to catch her breath. He figured they were up around 7500 feet, which was a little higher than the mare was used to operating. Finally, he came to the cleft in the solid wall of rock. With a little urging, he got the mare into it, and then came out on the other side.

Sure enough, there before him lay one of the greenest stretches of grassland he had ever seen. If a man couldn't make a living raising cattle on that kind of grass, he couldn't make a living doing anything. Longarm wondered why Ashton wanted to fool around with counterfeiting with such a beautiful setup. The pasture must have been fifteen to twenty thousand acres in size. It went on as far as he could see in the distance, with each side backed up to the mountains so that it was a natural enclosure. He could even see mountain streams leaping out of the rock and flowing down into the green grass. He didn't know if they were springs or late-melting snow. All he knew was here was a man with land and grass and water aplenty, and he was printing money that was worthless.

There was a trail of sorts to his right. He took it, and put the mare into a slow lope since the path was smooth and level. He didn't see anyone and didn't expect to see anyone, not for a ways at least. It was his understanding that it was about four or five miles to Ashton's headquarters. He had gone no more than a half mile when he heard a summons from above and just behind him. A voice called out, "Halt! Halt, you! On the horse, halt!"

Longarm pulled the mare to a slow stop, and then turned back in the saddle and looked up. Twenty yards up the side of the mountain, securely positioned behind several boulders, was a man wearing a big hat with a rifle pointed straight at Longarm.

Longarm said, "Don't get excited, fellow. I'm just here to see Mr. Ashton."

"What do you want to see him about?"

Longarm swiveled his head around to the front. A man

had come walking down from the side of a rocky outcropping, and had stepped out into the path directly in front of Longarm. He too was carrying a rifle.

Longarm said, "Well, right now, that's my business. Right now, I'm wondering why I'm getting met with rifles when I ain't done a damn thing. I'm just here on a business trip. What's all the artillery for?"

"We're just here to make sure you don't make too much noise," the man in front said. "Mr. Ashton doesn't like too much noise. We want to make sure you keep your business nice and quiet. You understand?"

Longarm nodded. "Yeah, I understand. I don't get it, but I understand. What happens now? Do I just sit here?"

The man in front shook his head and walked up to Longarm. "Turn over all your firearms," he said.

"Why should I do that?"

The man shrugged. "I don't give a damn if you do or not, but you're not going another foot toward Mr. Ashton's until you turn over all your firearms. And that means all of them. Any that you've got in your saddlebags, that one you got in your boot, and certainly that one in your holster. They'll be right here when you come back. That is, *if* you come back."

Longarm said, "What the hell is this all about? This is a hell of a way to be neighborly."

The man, who was about thirty and hard-faced, said, "We ain't trying to be neighborly. In fact, we ain't your neighbors. So either turn over the firearms, or get the hell out of here."

Longarm seemed to be considering, though he had already made up his mind to surrender his weapons. It didn't much matter to him one way or the other. All he wanted was to look the place over to see where he could penetrate

42

the defenses under the cover of darkness, some way to enter on the sly. He reached down, pulled his rifle out of the boot, and handed it to the hard-faced young man. He said, "That's a good rifle, and the sights were straight on it when I handed it to you. I'd like to get it back in the same shape."

The man nodded. "If they're straight, they'll be straight when you pick them up. You be straight with us and we'll be straight with you."

Longarm thought fleetingly about the badge he had left back at the hotel. He didn't think he should be completely straight with these gentlemen. He took his revolver out of his holster and handed it over. Then he turned in the saddle, opened one side of the saddlebags, took out the other revolver, and handed that over. He said, "Will that do it?"

"Is that all of them?"

Longarm didn't expect that the derringer in his buckle counted. "Ain't that enough?" he said.

The hard-faced man walked around to the left side of Longarm's horse. "Why don't you just step down and let's be sure you haven't forgotten something," he said. "It's real easy, as hot as this weather has been, to forget a gun or a knife. You might start by taking off your boots. Many a man forgets he's got a pistol in his boot."

Longarm stepped down and then sat down on the ground. He took off his boots, one at a time, and showed that they were empty. "This is the silliest damned thing I've ever seen," he said. "I'm going to talk business and you have me taking off my clothes."

"Well, put your boots back on and stand up. Put your hands over your head."

"What for?"

"You'll see."

While Longarm stood there with his hands over his head, the man patted him down for any concealed weapon. Thankfully, he didn't find the derringer inside Longarm's belt buckle.

Finally, the man motioned for Longarm to drop his arms. "All right. You look like you've passed the test. Mount up and ride on ahead."

"Where am I headed?"

The man nodded his head toward the long end of the pasture. He said, "You are headed that way. You don't have to worry about getting exact directions. You'll have somebody to help you out before you've gone too much further."

To emphasize the point, he gave Longarm's mare a slight slap on the rump with his hat. The horse started forward, but she was far too calm and too trail-wise to bolt. Longarm supposed it was the man's idea of a joke. He was just glad that the man didn't know that he had two .38-caliber shells that he might find good use for, maybe on the gentleman who liked to slap horses on their rump with his hat.

But it did make one thing clear to him—this was not going to be an easy place to slip up on. There had been guards on the southern side of the range in the rocks and the mountains and crevasses. He was willing to bet that, far across the pasture on the other side bordered by mountain peaks, there were an equal number of guards. He expected company at nearly any time. He expected that there were roaming guards all over the place. It made him angry just to think about it. Billy Vail was so damned free and easy with his assignments. It was just a shame that his boss didn't get to come along on such an assignment. And that damned fool of a Treasury Department man . . . Longarm decided that he would rather have the Treasury man riding alongside of him than to have his dressmaker lady friend, Pauline, in bed next to him. And that was saying a hell of a lot.

Longarm kept to the small wagon path that swept away from the mountainside and cut over into the center of the pasture. Very shortly, he could see several dots swinging his way from the northern side of the pasture. He was heading east, and he veered even further toward the north so it would appear to the gentlemen that were headed to intercept him that he was just as cooperative as all hell. The last thing he wanted was for anybody in that place where he was so badly outgunned to get the idea that he wasn't cooperating. The guards were not long in reaching his side. Two came in first, hard-looking young men who wore their revolvers set up for business. They also carried carbines and shotguns. Longarm wondered if the place had a few cannons just in case they got into a large-scale war. The two men were both very similar, but one was riding a pinto horse.

He said, "All right, mister, and what's your business?"

"My name is Curtis Long. I was passing through this area, and I heard that the gentleman that owns this spread was usually in the market for some good horseflesh. I thought I'd go and talk to him and see if we can do some business. I hadn't planned on being stopped and searched and generally hindered in my business."

A third man rode up. He sat back silently behind the other two and watched. Longarm had the feeling that he was some sort of foreman. He wore a black flat-crowned hat with a stiff flat brim.

The man on the pinto said, "We ain't hindering you, mister, but we've got our job to do, which is to make damned sure you've got real business on this spread and that you're not just here to cause mischief.''

Longarm gave him a frankly amazed look. ''So far, I've counted about five or six of you. You're all as well armed as if you were in the army. Now, would you mind telling me how in hell I could cause any mischief? I have the feeling that there's more of you out there.''

The man wearing the flat-crowned hat said, ''You've got that right, mister.''

Longarm looked past the other two at him. ''Got what right? That I ain't going to cause no mischief? Or that you all are well armed? There seems to be enough of you to fight off an army.''

The man smiled coldly and without humor. ''Whichever,'' he said.

The man riding the pinto turned around and looked at him. ''What shall I do, Clay?''

The man in the black hat gave a small shrug. ''Take him on up the line. Let Early decide if he should see the boss.''

The man on the pinto nodded. He looked at Longarm and said, ''Let's go, mister. Head it right in that direction.'' He pointed, and Longarm could just barely make out the dim outline of some buildings toward the east.

They rode, Longarm in the middle, and one of the two men on each side. The man on the pinto was on his left. Longarm said, ''Where are we headed?''

''Well, we are headed to find out if you're going to see Mr. Ashton. The straw boss will make that decision.''

''Why? Ain't that guy in the black hat the foreman?''

''He's one of them. But the man that he's talking about, Mr. Early, is higher than he is.''

''What do you all have? Ranks like you do in the army?''

The man on the pinto gave Longarm a hard long look. ''You sure ask a lot of questions, mister,'' he said.

The outlines of the house and the outbuildings that had been so dim in the distance were now becoming clear. Longarm was not particularly surprised at the size of the house. He had never seen a castle except in pictures in books, but he felt like he was looking at one as they rode closer and closer. He didn't know why a man needed that big a place to live in, except if he had a lot of wives. But since this wasn't Mormon country and he didn't figure that Brigham Young was who he was going to see, it still left him puzzled as to why a man would want to sink that much money into just a house. You could only sleep in one room and one bed at a time. You could only sit in one room and you could only eat in one room. So what he wanted with the rest of them, Longarm couldn't figure.

He saw a man leave one of the barns that lay some distance from the house. The man was mounted, and he came riding directly toward them. As he neared, Longarm could see that he was a man close to forty. If anything, maybe a little over it. He was wearing a blue suit of clothes, complete with vest and a four-in-hand tie. You didn't see that very often except with preachers.

Longarm said to man at his left, "Is this going to be the man that can say yes or no to my visit? I forgot what that fellow back there called him."

"Yes, that's Mr. Early. He can say yes or no to just about anything around here next to Mr. Ashton."

"Well, I hope we get along all right."

"If it were me, I'd see to it."

By now, they had slowed their horses, and pulled them to a stop as the man in the suit came riding up. To his surprise, Longarm saw that he was slightly portly and had a genial face. His head was topped by a pearl-gray, narrow-brimmed Stetson hat. He looked like he'd be more at home behind a desk than on the deck of a cow horse.

The man to Longarm's left said respectfully, "Good day, Mr. Early. Got a visitor to the place. We've got to ask your permission about him."

The genial-looking man glanced at Longarm and half smiled. He said, "The name is Joel Early. And who might you be, sir?"

Longarm said, "My name is Custis Long. I'm in the high-class horseflesh business. Sometimes, I even handle blooded stock. I was passing through the town of Silverton and I heard that Mr. Ashton was sometimes in the market for good horses. I've got them and I will sell them, but these gentlemen here don't want me to go directly up there." He paused and glanced to his left and then to his right. "I don't know exactly why, but it appears that I need your permission."

Early laughed slightly. "Aw, that's just the way these old boys are, you know. Kind of the way the boss wants it. Mr. Ashton is a busy man, and he's a wealthy man. I don't mind you knowing that, even though you're trying to sell him something. If we just let any Tom, Dick, and Harry come riding on this place, well, there would be a line out his front door and plumb on up here to where we are standing. So, I kind of make a selection of who I let go in to see him and who doesn't. Sound about right to you?"

Longarm was doing his best to appear to be a horse trader. He said, "Well, sure. You've got to keep the ribbon clerks out. I can see that. It makes sense if the man is busy and has important work to do. I figured that the people that I sell to are just as busy and just as important, and I don't have to go through a receiving line to get to see *them*. If you take my meaning."

Early still looked congenial. "Well, you'll just have to

forgive us for the way we do things. You say you've got good blooded stock, is that correct?"

"Yes, sir! I do! I've got some horses with some Kentucky blood in them, some with thoroughbred in them. I've even got some good quarter horses."

"And where would all these horses be, Mr. Long? Was that the correct name?"

"Yes, sir. That's my name. These horses are in Oregon. I'm on my way there now. I was just passing through on the train and got off to take a rest, and heard about this roost up here and thought I'd come investigate it."

Early nodded his head at the gray mare. He said, "Is that an example of the kind of blood stock you are talking about?"

Longarm laughed appreciatingly. "Well, no, sir. No, sir. Of course not. This is just my own personal horse, one of several that I use. She is a using horse. She's gentle and calm and, besides that, she likes to ride the train. So, when I've sold all the other horses I brought, I still have her to get around on. If I hadn't had her this morning when I got up, I'd have had to rent a horse or I'd have had to walk out here."

Early chuckled. "Well, that makes right good sense to me. Now me, I'm not much of a horse man. I don't know the bloodlines, don't know all the finer points, if you take my meaning, Mr. Long. But I will warn you that Mr. Ashton is. From time to time, he has raised horses. So, you want to be on your toes when you talk to him about horseflesh. It's a subject he does know."

"Does that mean that I can go and see him?"

Early looked at the two men with Longarm. He said, "I don't see why a gentleman in the horse business shouldn't be allowed to see Mr. Ashton. Do ya'll?"

49

Both of the men answered in unison. "No, sir. Not if you say so, Mr. Early."

"Well then, why don't you take the gentleman up there and help him in to see Mr. Ashton?"

The man to Longarm's left said, "We'll tend to that, Mr. Early. Thank you, sir."

They put the spurs to their horses almost simultaneously and started forward at a slow lope. Longarm glanced back. The man in the blue suit was just sitting his horse, watching them as they headed for the house. Somehow it gave him an uneasy feeling.

Chapter 4

A Chinese man in a white coat and what looked to Longarm to be velvet shoes let him in the big wooden front door. Longarm walked into a long hall with polished floors and pictures hung on the walls. He had expected nothing less, for as they had ridden up to the front of the house, he'd been struck by its size. It was built mostly from natural rock, and appeared to be two-storied and at least a hundred and fifty feet long, maybe that much deep. Standing in the hallway, he could see a curved staircase running around the wall to the upstairs. The two men that had been with him had stayed outside, settling down on the steps to smoke and wait for him to come back out. One of them had warned him to watch his manners.

He'd added, ''I wouldn't be lighting up no cigarettes or cigars without being asked to, and I wouldn't be pouring myself any of that good whiskey Mr. Ashton keeps. If he wants you to have it, he'll give it to you.''

The houseboy had disappeared, and Longarm stood cooling his heels in the big hall, looking around him. There was a set of double doors to his immediate left. It was through these that the man had disappeared. To the right, Longarm

51

could look through a large opening and see a sitting room, and then beyond that what appeared to be a dining room, and then beyond that what appeared to be another sitting room. He reckoned the bedrooms and whatnot were upstairs. He wondered if the bathrooms were indoors. That was a luxury that very few people in the country could enjoy, but it made sense to him that somebody making his own money would probably be able to afford it.

Longarm kept sweeping his gaze around, noticing the pictures on the wall, noticing the fine drapes. The man had built a lovely place, and Longarm wondered who he enjoyed it with. A place like this couldn't very well be enjoyed by one's own self.

A movement caught his eye, and he looked upwards toward the top of the stairs. Just behind the banister off the top story, he caught sight of a woman. She moved almost as soon as he raised his eyes, but he had seen enough to tell that she was a dark-haired beauty with a trace of Spanish blood in her. She had on some kind of dress made out of flowered material. It had only been a second, but he'd seen the bare shoulders and a smooth, lightly tanned bosom beneath the bodice of her gown. But all too quickly she had disappeared. He took a step in the direction of the stairs, but just then the door opened and the Chinese houseboy was back. He motioned Longarm toward the room. ''You come. You come see big boss. He see you, fellow.''

Longarm stepped past him, taking off his hat as he did. Hell, he didn't like taking off his hat, but he was posing as a man selling horses, and that was what a horse trader would do if he was in a rich man's house.

Longarm walked into what he took to be a library—at least it had enough books to make one. He stopped halfway into the big room and looked around for someone or something he could report to. Just then, the small Chinese man came scuttling by him, went to the far wall, and opened another door. He motioned to Longarm. He said, "You come, please."

Longarm walked past him, this time into what was clearly an office. There, against the big double window, was a long desk, and behind the desk was a man.

The man was writing with a pen on a piece of paper. He took a moment to finish, blotted his work, and then put his pen down before looking up at Longarm. He said, "Yes? My name is Vernon Ashton."

Longarm walked forward to the desk. He didn't offer to sit down, although there were two chairs available. He said, "My name is Custis Long. I'm in the horse business."

The man leaned back in his chair. "Oh, that's interesting. I am interested in horses. I like horses. I like to race horses. I like to own horses. I like to see my men mounted on good horses. Do you have good horses, Mr. Long?"

Longarm said, "I sure do." He was surprised at the look of his host. Vernon Ashton was a small, delicate, middle-aged man with graying hair at the temples. He was wearing an open-necked silk shirt with a suede vest. It was clear that he was not a man who had ever done much hard work in his life. His skin looked as soft as a woman's. His teeth were white and even.

Vernon Ashton said, "Why don't you sit down and tell me about your horses? You must have impressed Mr. Early."

"Why? Because I got by him?"

Ashton laughed in a good-humored way. "Yes. That and the fact that Mr. Early knows a great deal about horses. He wouldn't have let you in to see me if you didn't also seem to know a great deal about horses. Tell me, what kind of horses do you handle?''

Longarm settled into an upholstered armchair. He said, ''Well, I've got several grades. I've got your common saddle horse, good for range work. Some of them are good for a ride in the park and some of them are good traveling horses. I've got your higher-blooded stock that your gentlemen can ride when they go to church or to the saloon, whichever place they care to go. Then I've got some fine-blooded stock, high-stepping some of them, some of them just plain fast.''

Vernon Ashton nodded slowly. ''That's very descriptive, but it hardly tells me about your stock. Where, by the way, do you do business?''

Longarm crossed his legs. ''I do business mostly out of my head, wherever I am. I keep my stock in Oregon at a small place called Medford. I was on my way back—I've been down south of here—and I stopped off and heard about you. I thought I'd come and see if I had anything you might be interested in having a look at.''

''So, your stock's in Oregon? You have nothing to show me now?''

Longarm shook his head. ''No, and besides that, it would have been impossible for me to have known what you were looking for.''

''That's true enough.''

''What would you be looking for?''

''I'm looking for blooded stock. Perhaps racing stock. Tell me, do you have any Morgan thoroughbred crosses?''

Longarm slapped his knee. ''Happens I do! Got several. Got a couple of geldings and a mare, and I also have a stud.''

"You did understand me to say Morgan thoroughbred crosses, is that correct?"

"Of course I did. I have some quarter-horse thoroughbred crosses, and I have some Morgan thoroughbred crosses."

"You've got thoroughbred Morgan crosses? Tell me, what kind of animal did that produce?"

Longarm was getting in deep water on the blooded stock. He was a veteran stock trader, but he generally didn't get into those kinds of high-class animals. He wasn't sure he'd ever seen a Morgan thoroughbred cross. He'd seen Morgans and he'd seen thoroughbreds at race meets, but he had never seen a cross. But he knew that a Morgan was a stayer, and he knew that a thoroughbred was fast, so he said, "Well, you get a stayer with a lot of speed."

Ashton looked amused. "Is that right?"

"Yes, sir. That's a fact."

Ashton said "Tell me, Mr. Long. Who have you sold horses to that I might know?"

Longarm felt distinctly more and more uncomfortable. He thought he might have picked a better disguise than that of a horse trader, but he had traded so many horses that it had seemed natural. His mistake had been allowing the talk to creep into such high-and-mighty bloodlines as Morgans and thoroughbreds and crosses and crosses thereof, of which he knew very little.

He said, "Well, sir, I can't say exactly who you might know." His mind raced as he racked his memory trying to think of some rich men in the area that he could name, though he actually didn't know if any of them were interested in high-blooded horses. He named a couple of mine owners down in Las Cruces, New Mexico, that he had helped out. He named a prominent banker in Denver, and

55

then was promptly rattled that he would name a banker to a supposed counterfeiter. After that, he pulled back and thought of a couple of ranchers in the lower part of Colorado that he knew fairly well. Finally, he ended up saying, "I'm not a really big operation, Mr. Ashton. I'm what you might call a custom service. You tell me what you want and I'll go out and find it and sell it to you at a fair price."

Ashton chuckled again and his eyes narrowed. "By the way," he said, "I observed you as you came up to the house. That's a nice-looking gray mare you are riding. Is she a Morgan thoroughbred cross?"

Longarm almost blushed. "Oh, my heavens, no. That old girl is just a using horse that I keep around to take with me when I'm delivering or picking up horses. She's gentle and handles well and doesn't cause me any trouble."

Ashton sat forward. "I see." There was something about his eyes that seemed to have changed. They seemed narrower, a little harder. He reached out and rang a bell, and in less than a half moment, the Chinese man came shuffling into the room. Ashton said, "Lei Chang, take this gentleman back out. Send in one of the riders that's out there. I want to give him some instructions."

He stood and put out his hand. "Thank you for coming, Mr. Long. Perhaps we can do some business. Be sure and give your address or how I can reach you to one of my riders. They will see that I get it."

Longarm shook the small white soft hand that was offered, trying to be careful not to squeeze too hard. He wondered why Ashton didn't write down how he could be reached himself, but he supposed that wasn't how business was done by rich people who counterfeited twenty-dollar bills.

He thanked Ashton for his time, and then turned and

followed the Chinese man out through the door through the library, then into the hall, and then out the front door. The Chinese man spoke rapidly to the rider that had been on the pinto horse. He disappeared quickly inside the house.

Longarm turned to the other man. "What the hell is going on?" he said.

The man shrugged. "Beats the hell out of me. Apparently Mr. Ashton wants to talk to him."

"What are you fellows' names?"

"It's none of your business, but his name is Steve and my name—I guess is George. I guess that's good enough."

Longarm said, "Well, there ain't no use getting huffy about it. I didn't mean to be sticking my nose into your business. I just thought it would be handy to know what to call you. I think I might be coming back out."

"Well, there is always a chance of that, I reckon."

In a few minutes, the man on the pinto horse, now identified as Steve, was back. Without a word, he motioned for them to mount up. In a few moments, they were riding back toward the way they had come. Longarm looked, but he didn't see the man in the blue suit, Joel Early.

As they rode along, Steve dropped back and motioned for George to join him. He waved Longarm ahead. "You go on," he said. "Take it slow. We'll catch up with you. I think my horse has got a rock in his shoe."

"Need some help with it?"

"No, you just go on. Take it slow."

Longarm rode on, glancing back over his shoulder. He could see them talking. He didn't see them fooling with either of the horses' hooves. He had had a funny feeling ever since he had seen that look on Ashton's face. The feeling had grown stronger when Steve was sent for, and now it was getting stronger and stronger. Something was wrong, and it wasn't going to get right any time soon.

He stopped his horse and waited until Steve and George had mounted up and caught up with him. "Anything wrong other than your horse's hoof?" he said.

Steve said, "No, we just need to be getting along. Let's move it on up a notch."

They put their horses into a trot, and then into a slow lope. They went that way about two miles before Steve abruptly pulled his horse down. He said, speaking past Longarm, who was riding in the middle, "George, why don't you ride on ahead and see if those boys are ready for us. They're liable to be up there in the rocks. They need to escort Mr. Long on out of here. Why don't you tear on off up there?"

For answer, the other rider nodded, applied spurs to his horse, and rode on ahead at a hard gallop.

Longarm watched as he topped the slight rise and then went over on the other side. He said casually, "He seemed to be in a hell of a hurry."

"Oh, I don't reckon he's hurrying. He would just like to get on back and get some vittles, just like I would. It's getting on about that time. You'll probably make your noon meal in town, won't you?"

"Yeah, I reckon I will," Longarm said. His eyes were shifting back and forth, seeing where the different men were, wondering what was coming next. He was down to one derringer and two cartridges. He didn't like the odds with so many people around. He also could not shake the feeling that something very definitely was going on that meant him no good. He thought it had started with Ashton when he'd called the one named Steve back in the house and given him some kind of message. That message was now being carried on to the two men who had initially disarmed him.

He could not imagine what mistake he had made, but something had given him away. Maybe the man had recognized his name, that of Custis Long. But if he'd been a real federal marshal, the real Custis Long, he wouldn't have gone in there giving his correct name. Not many people knew him by anything except Longarm. Not many of the wrong kind of people, that is.

They were making a pretty good time of it, jogging along at a high trot. Now, Longarm could see that George was coming back his way. He just nodded at Steve as he came up. "I'm heading back into the camp house," he said. "The boys up ahead are ready for you."

Steve said, "Go on ahead."

As George rode off, Longarm glanced sideways at the rider. "What did he mean, they are ready for me?"

Steve shrugged innocently. "Hell, I don't know what he meant by it. Got your guns ready for you, near as I could tell. Why, are you worried about something?"

"No, should I be?"

Steve spat over the side of his horse. "Not that I know of."

In a few minutes, Longarm could see ahead that the two men who had been on guard up in the rocks had now come down and were mounted on horses. They rode slowly forward as Longarm and Steve came up. When they got within a few yards, the bigger of the two men, a broad-shouldered man wearing a gray slouch hat and a checkered shirt, said to Steve, "You can go on back now. We'll see him out."

Longarm said mildly, "Where did you get the horses?"

The man in the checkered shirt said carelessly, "Why, you don't reckon we go around here on foot, do you?

59

Plenty of places around here to tie up a horse in the shade. No need for you to worry about that. You just ride on along with us and we'll show you off the property.''

Longarm glanced back to see Steve heading back to the ranch headquarters at a fast clip. He said, ''What about my firearms? When do I get my guns back?''

''Oh, we are going to see to that right soon. Ain't we, Ernie?''

Ernie was the man on Longarm's right. He said, ''Yep, good fellow like this here horse trader, can't be too nice to a man like that. Can we, Charlie? We're going to give him his guns back. Maybe even a little something besides.''

Longarm said, ''You fellows seem to be in a mighty good humor this morning.''

The man in the checkered shirt said, ''How come we shouldn't be in a good humor? Good pay, light work, and the vittles are good. Do you know anything else a man needs besides that?''

Ernie said with a laugh, ''That and an occasional visit to town to see the ladies over at the saloon.''

Charlie snickered. ''Yeah, there is that,'' he said.

They had passed the place where Longarm had been disarmed, and were now approaching the cleft in the wall that seemed to separate the ranch. The ground was rising slowly as they headed that way.

Longarm said, ''If you boys just want to give me my weapons, I can see my way out of here without much trouble.''

Charlie said, ''Oh, that's all right. We'll go on just a little bit further with you.''

Longarm said, ''I hate to see you go through this much trouble.''

Charlie said, ''Like I said, that's all right.'' A few yards further on, Longarm was conscious that the men who had been riding with him had pulled back. He was suddenly alone. He immediately stopped, and whirled his horse around. The two men were behind him, perhaps ten yards away. They were both holding revolvers.

Longarm said, "What the hell is this all about?"

Charlie dismounted, never letting his gun waver from Longarm's chest. He said, "Well, we thought you might enjoy climbing up the side of this mountain and we're going to help you do it."

"I don't see the point of that," Longarm said.

Ernie also dismounted, and walked forward a few paces, holding his revolver in his hand. He said, "Well, son, I don't think you got much choice. We don't think you are a horse trader. We don't know what your business was here, but Mr. Ashton didn't care for it. Now, we're going to have to take you out of here the hard way. Now, get down off that mare and let's get started up the side of this bunch of rocks here."

Longarm watched them narrowly. They both handled their revolvers as if they knew how to use them. But they were too far away for him to use his only weapon, the derringer. He let his horse close a little more of the distance before he pulled the mare to a stop.

Charlie said, "Now, do you understand? Get down off that horse, son. We're liable to have to let some light into you right here and now. I don't think you'd care for that. If you get up there amongst those rocks, you might have a chance on getting away from us."

"Are you planning on doing what I think you are going to do?"

"This ain't nothing to do with us, understand? This is

just orders. We take orders from the man who pays us, and you've gotten wrong with him.''

Longarm still sat his horse. ''Well, do me one favor then, if you can. Would you mind telling me what I did that got him so convinced that I'm not a horse trader?''

The two men half smiled at each other. ''What do you say, Charlie? Do you reckon it would be all right to tell him?''

''I don't see why not. I don't reckon he's going to be using that trick much longer.''

Ernie said, ''We'll tell you if you'll tell us who you really are.''

Longarm said, ''That's a square deal.''

''Well, who are you? What is your real business?''

''After a fashion, I am in the horse business. I'm a horse thief and I wanted on to this place to look it over and see what I could make off with.''

It seemed to strike the two riders as very funny. They both laughed and slapped their legs. Ernie said, ''Well, that does make sense. That beats all. Comes in here pretending to be a horse trader, going to take off with our stock. You were going to trade, all right, but you weren't going to give us nothing.''

''That was about the size of it.''

''And now you want to know what you done, is that it?''

''Yeah.''

Ernie said, ''Well, you made one slipup. There ain't no such thing as a Morgan and a thoroughbred crossed. I don't know what kind of horse you'd get out of it, but Mr. Ashton doesn't believe he wants one. Now, why don't you just step on down off that horse and let's get on with the business at hand?''

Longarm was judging the distance between them. Once

62

he was on the ground, there would be no more than five yards separating him from the pair. He felt comfortable with the distance, but he thought he could make it even better. Very carefully, with his right hand working under his belt buckle, he swung his leg over the rump of the horse and stepped down to the ground, taking his left foot out of the stirrup as he did. He released his left hand from the saddle horn and slowly turned. The derringer was already in his hand and he cocked the hammer as he coughed slightly. He was holding the hand just behind his right leg. With a nonchalant air, he stepped with his left leg toward the two men and then seemed to stumble. He was not stumbling, though, he was simply going to his knee. As he did, he brought his right arm up swiftly, the derringer buried in his hand. Before they realized their danger, he had shot Ernie in the chest with the top barrel, and then fired and hit Charlie in the stomach.

They both went down with surprised looks on their faces. The pistols tumbled from their hands. Longarm knew he had to work fast. The shots would have been noticed— there were too many riders not to have heard them. He stooped quickly and grabbed up the two revolvers the men had been holding, and shoved them in his belt. Until he found his own, he needed to be armed. He went to the saddlebags of Charlie's horse and swiftly lifted up the flap. Both of his revolvers were inside. He could see that the boot on Ernie's horse contained his Winchester. There was a boot on both sides that carried a shotgun in one side and a rifle in the other. As quickly as he could, he took his two revolvers, holding them in one hand by the trigger guards, and then ran around and pulled his Winchester from the boot.

He looked back over his shoulder. He could see riders

in the distance, but they were too far away to tell if they were headed toward him or were simply patroling. He wasted no time. As fast as he could, he went back to his horse and shoved the Winchester home in its own boot. He pitched the two revolvers of the two men down on the ground. Then he put his spare back in his saddlebags and swung aboard the mare. He could tell that one of the men was dead. The one he had shot in the stomach, Charlie, was still alive. He was moaning for help.

Longarm said, "I hope you get some, neighbor. Just like you gave me. No hard feelings, by the way. I was just following the orders of the man who pays me. Wasn't that what you said? You were just doing your job. You were just going to march me up there in those rocks and shoot me in the back of the head. Wasn't that about it?"

On the ground, Charlie looked up at him with pleading eyes, his hands holding the spreading blood from his stomach wound. In a croaking voice, he said, "Need water. Water."

Longarm glanced back toward the horsemen. He couldn't see any headed directly toward him. He rode over to the first horse he saw with a canteen and took it off the saddle horn. He unscrewed the cap and then leaning down, lowered it to Charlie, who caught it with one hand. He poured it in his mouth.

Longarm watched him. "You know, you ain't supposed to do that when you get shot in the stomach," he said, "But then, in your case, I don't reckon it matters much. I've got to tell you something, Charlie. You all have pretty well pissed me off. So has Ashton. I don't take kindly to the way you have treated me, the whole bunch of you. And when it comes down to it, I might not forgive and forget, if you catch my drift."

Charlie made a gurgling sound. The water that was bubbling out of his mouth seemed stained with pink. Longarm wondered if the shot from the derringer had nicked a lung. It was amazing how much power that little gun had. It didn't jump much in your hand, but it did slam back. You could hide the whole thing in your hands, fire between your fingers, and the man on the receiving end wouldn't know what had hit him until it was too late.

Longarm lifted his reins and said, "Well, Charlie, I've got to get going. I hope somebody finds you in time. I don't reckon there will be anybody to tell the law that you and Ernie got shot by a man like me, but if there is, we're going to have to have an investigation. I don't think Ashton wants this place investigated too close, do you?"

Charlie's eyes were starting to glaze over. Longarm gave him a salute, not knowing whether he could see it or not. He touched the spurs to his mare and put her into a fast walk as he entered the little break in the rocks and began picking his way off Ashton's property.

When Longarm was clear of the mountain, he was out onto the level plain that he had crossed before. In the distance, he could see the town. He could see the smoke curling out of the chimneys and from the cooking houses. He put the mare into a trot, and then into a slow lope. She'd had about fifteen miles of work that day, and didn't need to be used too hard. She also had not had any water. So far as that went, he hadn't had anything to drink himself. He had not brought any of his Maryland whiskey along for the very good reason that he was afraid that he might have lost it—either getting spilled or shot, he didn't know which.

As he rode, he speculated on the chances of someone from the ranch lodging a complaint with the sheriff—if the town of Silverton even had a sheriff or any kind of law.

For the reasons he'd told Charlie, he doubted such a thing would happen. There would have to be an investigation. If it came to that, he'd pull out his marshal's badge and put a stop to any foolishness. But he didn't think it would come to that. He thought Ashton would be perfectly willing to write off two gunhands rather than ask for more trouble.

Longarm had not lied about the situation making him angry. Ashton had just carelessly and callously and casually sent word to have him killed. Longarm had known men who would kill, had known men who had killed. But he had never seen one quite as cool about it as Ashton. Longarm might as well have been a spider or an ant or some other kind of insect the way Ashton had gone about stamping a boot on him. It made him mad as hell. He wasn't a man who let anger affect his job or any of his emotions so far as that went. He had come into this assignment reluctantly, and he was still reluctant in some ways, but now he was personally involved. He was determined to get Vernon Ashton. The very nerve of the man made him angry and determined to even the score. He was interested in seeing how Ashton acted when *he* was personally threatened. Longarm intended to give how to do that a great deal of thought.

He rode his horse to the hotel livery stable, then turned the mare over to the stable boy and walked on down to the front of the hotel. He was surprised to see, by the clock in the lobby, that it was no more than a quarter to one. So much had happened that it seemed that it should have been much later. His stomach was reminding him that it had not been attended to in some while, so he headed in to the dining room. He had intended to do some hard thinking while he ate, but he saw Finley sitting alone at a window table, and he made his way there and pulled out a chair.

Finley looked up, a light smile playing on his face. He

said, "Well, here's the horse trader. Been out and about this morning, have you?"

Longarm shrugged. "You might say that. Don't have any good whiskey on you, do you?"

"Got some in my room."

"So do I, but I'm too damned tired to go get it," Longarm said. "I'll just drink what the waiter will bring us. Care for a drink?"

Finley shook his head and pointed to his coffee. "A little early in the day for me just yet."

Longarm said, "I've never seen a bottle of whiskey yet that had the face of a clock on it."

Finley chuckled. "All right. It's a little too early in the day for my constitution. How's that? Tell me, did you do any trading this morning?"

Just then the waiter came up, and Longarm ordered a bottle of whiskey and a steak with all the trimmings to go with it. He said, "And tell that cook that I don't want that steak beat to death. Just put a good rope burn on it."

When the waiter had left, Longarm said, "Oh, I scattered around a little." He wasn't anxious to speak of his adventures at Ashton's place. As a matter of fact, he intended to deny that he had ever been on the place at all.

He said, "I didn't do much good, so other than riding around a little bit looking at some of the mines, I ain't got much to say. How about yourself?"

Finley said, "Well, I think it's just about time for that pasture of mine. I think this next spring I'm going to be turning cattle in on it. I'm bringing some cattle up from Texas to winter. It's going to make a mighty good grass crop."

Longarm was about to say something, but the waiter arrived with his whiskey and his glass. He poured himself out a shot, and then held the bottle toward an empty glass in front of Finley. He said, ''Are you sure you won't change your mind?''

Finley frowned slightly, but then nodded. ''Well, why not? Hell, I'll just imagine that it's later in the day than it is.''

Longarm poured them both out a drink, and they toasted to luck and then both knocked the whiskey back. It felt good to Longarm, going down in his stomach. It relaxed him and warmed him. Sometimes whiskey could be a good friend, nearly as good as a woman, but not quite. His mind drifted back to the woman he had seen upstairs at Ashton's. She had been a real beauty. A little Spanish maybe. He wondered what she was to Ashton. He guessed Ashton to be about fifty years old. He would have asked Finley, but he knew the man would just say that he knew nothing about the place. That made Longarm a little more than curious. If *he* was a constant visitor to such a place as Silverton, and if an operation like Ashton's was going on, *he* damned sure would be more than curious.

But Longarm said, ''Well, I reckon then you'll be looking to start plowing for next year. That about right?''

Finley said, ''Well, I've got some dynamiting work to do first. A few rock ledges are in the wrong place.''

Longarm was surprised. ''Dynamiting? I didn't know that was part of the cattle business.''

Finley nodded. ''Yeah, in this part of the country, a man uses dynamite damned near the same as he'd use a plow or a shovel, so it ain't no big operation. Of course, you'll see a few folks around here missing a finger or two or even a hand. Most folks are familiar with the stuff anyway. Haven't you noticed the booms that go off every once in a while? Those are from the mines. They're pretty routine.''

Longarm narrowed his eyes, thinking. He said, a little distractedly, "Yeah, I have noticed that noise. I guess they are blowing holes in these mountains at a pretty steady rate."

"Something like that. Listen, Mr. Long, I've got to be running along. I'll maybe see you tonight for poker?"

"Sounds good to me," said Longarm.

After Finley left, Longarm sat back in his chair, lit a cigarillo, and stared at the window, thinking that he was going to get back at Vernon Ashton for certain. The only question now was how. He kind of halfway thought that dynamite might play some kind of part in it. As far as he could tell, as badly as he was outnumbered by Ashton's men, he needed something to even up the score. Something powerful. He reckoned dynamite was about the most powerful thing near to hand. He didn't know if the Treasury Department would approve of what he had in mind. But he didn't think he was going to mention it to them. At least not until it was too late to matter.

Longarm ate his steak, and then paid his score at the table and went back to his room. He had a window that faced the mountains where the Ashton spread lay. He put a chair in front of the window and rested his arms on the back of the chair, his chin on his arms. He sat there staring at the hard rocky mountains that sheltered that beautiful high-plains prairie and the lovely valley. He thought and he thought, and then he thought some more. Finally, he made up his mind. He got up, went out of the hotel, and walked around town, moving up one street and then back down the opposite side. The town wasn't big enough that you'd miss much during a twenty-minute stroll. There were two general mercantile stores and one hardware store. He went into the hardware store and asked the man if they carried dynamite.

The clerk was wearing green garters and a green eye-shade. He looked almost startled at Longarm's question. "I reckon you must be a stranger in these parts," he said. "Hell, even the grocery store carries dynamite. Yeah, I've got dynamite. Where is your wagon? I'll load you up."

Longarm said, "How does it come?"

"By the case. That's the smallest amount you can buy. There's forty sticks to a case. How many cases do you want?"

Longarm said, "Well, I ain't planning on blowing the mountains down. I just got a little work to do on a small claim I have. Doesn't amount to a hill of beans. Can a man pay for two cases and just take one with him?"

"Yeah, we can arrange that. What about blasting caps? You'll need them. Do you know anything about blasting caps?"

Longarm scratched his head. "Well, I know considerable about a lot of things, but not as well as I need to. Maybe you better explain what a blasting cap is."

The clerk gave him a funny look. "Mister, are you sure you want to go out and fool with this stuff? These ain't Fourth of July firecrackers, you understand?"

"Well, you see, I've got this claim kind of hid off back in the country. I'd just as soon tend to it myself."

The clerk ducked down beneath the counter, and came up with several red sticks of dynamite and a few little apparatuses that looked like buttons, only they weren't made out of button material. He held one up. "This here is a blasting cap. You take your fuse and stick it in this, and then you crimp it into the end of your dynamite. You don't set the dynamite off with the fuse like you might think.

70

This here blasting cap will explode from the fuse. When it goes, that's what makes the dynamite explode. So if you ain't got a blasting cap in the stick of dynamite you're going to explode, it ain't going to go off.''

Longarm looked puzzled. ''What if you wanted to set off five or six sticks at once. Would you need a blasting cap and fuse in every one of them?''

The clerk said, ''No, just one will be enough. You tie them together real stout with string or even some tape we've got for that very purpose. When that one stick goes off, it sets the rest of them off and first thing you know, you've got a hell of a bang. But now, neighbor, this stuff is dangerous. You don't want to be standing around the corner when you set it off.''

''I reckon I can understand that,'' Longarm said. ''I reckon I'll take two cases, and how do those blasting caps come?''

''They come a dozen to a box and your fuse cord comes by the foot. It's five cents a foot, and I'll tell you what, it won't ever hurt to have more than enough fuse cord. You ain't ever going to get yourself blown up by having too much fuse cord. It's the fellow that tries to use too little that generally finds out what a rock feels like when it hits him in the face.''

Longarm said, ''Well then, I reckon I'll take fifty feet of fuse cord and a couple boxes of those blasting caps. I'm going to pay you for two cases of dynamite plus this other stuff, but I am going to leave one case with you. I don't think I can tote it all in one lump, not having a wagon.''

The clerk said, ''Well, my name is Ed. Your dynamite will be here when you get ready for it. I live above the store, so if you need it in the middle of the night, you can come knock on the door.''

The total came to $32.10. Longarm laid out the money and got a receipt. Billy Vail liked receipts. It made him a lot easier to get along with when you totaled up your cost of doing business.

Longarm didn't do much the rest of the day, and that night he had supper at the hotel. He didn't see Finley. He wondered where his friendly-faced acquaintance was taking his meal. About eight o'clock, he strolled over to the saloon, had a few drinks, and then found a seat in a poker game. Again, Finley was missing. Longarm played without much interest until about eleven o'clock. It was a game with lower stakes than he liked to play in. You couldn't protect your hand when everyone just sat and drew cards. They couldn't be run out with a big bet. To him, that wasn't poker, it was just silly.

He was glad enough to quit early anyway. He had plans for the next day, and he figured to be early to bed. He had one last drink at the bar, and then walked back around to his hotel. Just as he stepped back into the lobby, he saw Finley disappearing up the stairs. He started to call to him, but decided that it would be best to just spend the rest of the time by himself.

Back in his room, Longarm took the top off the case of dynamite, and contemplated just how to go about what he had planned. It was a plan with several stages, and what he had in mind for the next day was just sort of an opening bet—a very small opening bet. To begin with, he took four sticks of dynamite and taped them together. The sales clerk had been right about the tape. It did a much better job of holding the sticks together than string would have done. After that, he took his knife and cut off two feet of the fuse cord. He ran one end into the blasting cap and set it near the four sticks. He wasn't about to crimp that blasting cap into the dynamite until just before he was ready to use it.

He took four more sticks, only this time, he cut the fuse cord four feet long. Again, he inserted it into one of the blasting caps, and again just laid it on top of the dynamite. He had brought his saddlebags in from the livery stable, and he intended to see how much dynamite he could carry in them. As best as Longarm could figure, it looked to be about two dozen sticks, though he wasn't going to take that much on his first trip.

His next bundle was six sticks and this time, he cut the blasting cord six feet long. Then he tied up a bundle of eight sticks. It was bulky and lethal-looking. It almost scared him to handle so much power. But for all the talk around town, he wouldn't be surprised if every man in the hotel didn't have a case of dynamite just sitting around. Certainly no one had even glanced at him when he walked back through the lobby with it from the hardware store.

Once Longarm was satisfied with his load, he began packing it into his saddlebags. The two fours and the six-stick package fit well in one side of the saddlebags. The eight-stick bundle took up nearly all the room, outside of his spare six-gun, in the other side. It made him a little nervous having all that dynamite and all those blasting caps all wadded in together, but he figured it would be safe enough. The man at the hardware store had made it clear that the blasting caps would not go off without fire from the fuse cord. He damned sure wasn't going to strike any matches around them. The clerk at the store had reassured him that he could jostle it or shovel it around or mash it or stomp on it, and it still wouldn't explode.

Longarm set the saddlebags handy by the door, and then had a long drink of his Maryland whiskey. He measured the bottle to see how much he had left.

His mind still wasn't sure he was doing the right thing. He was going to make an early morning attack, somewhere between four and five o'clock, maybe even a little later than that. He knew it would be awfully quiet at that hour and any noise he made would be magnified. But also, he figured there would be fewer guards and less chance of him being seen. It seemed to him that it was a better idea than trying to pull the stunt off at four in the afternoon or six or ten at night. Besides, he wanted to be back at the hotel and in his bed once the excitement started.

It was solid dark when Longarm woke. He struck a match to look at his watch. It read ten minutes until four. That was close enough for his purposes. With very little effort, he shrugged into his clothes and pulled his boots on, and then strapped on his gun belt, made sure the derringer was in place, and then put on his hat. After that, he shouldered his saddlebags, picked up his winchester, and opened the door. The lobby was dark, and there seemed to be no one behind the desk. That suited him just fine.

He went out the front door of the hotel and skirted around to the livery stable. The boy who was supposed to be minding the place was asleep on a hay bale. Longarm set his saddle blanket and saddle on the back of the gray mare, and then led her quietly out of the livery stable. He hated to use the animal again so soon, but he thought the bay gelding might be a little too excitable for the work he had planned.

The town was sleeping. He saw no one about. He walked behind the first line of buildings where he would be out of sight, and then saddled the mare by cinching her up tight and tying on the saddlebags. That clerk might have said that no amount of jostling would set off the explosives, but he wasn't going to be any too careless with it. He put his

rifle home in the boot, swung aboard, and then set off toward the direction of Ashton's place.

At a slow trot, it was a two-mile ride to the foot of the
little mountains that ringed the place. You couldn't call
them mountains. They were really crags and buttes and tips
from other rock piles that had been there in the past. They
led up and into the gigantic Rockie Mountains, but these
were just the early steps. Nevertheless, they were an obsta-
cle to be reckoned with and one not so small.

As Longarm rode, he looked back toward the town. Even
in the morning dark, the town still looked asleep. He was
satisfied that he had left unnoticed by anyone except the
few town dogs that were lounging around the street. Not
that it made any difference. He really didn't particularly
care if any one had seen him. It would be very difficult to
connect his early morning departure with events that would
happen later on in the day.

After a few more minutes' ride, Longarm could see,
through the gray of the fading night, the cleft of the opening
in the crag that was the entrance to Ashton's place. He rode
almost to it so as to get his bearings, and then turned to his
right to circle the little line of foothills that stood like a
picket fence around the high-plains pasture. He was going
in a direction that he took to be southerly.

Longarm rode for approximately a half mile, calculating
that on the other side of the rocks was about where he had
been stopped by Charlie and Ernie, who had disarmed him.
Apparently that was a lookout position. He went on a little
further, searching for a little easier line of country where
there might be passage for his horse.

Finally, about a mile from the entrance, he found a small
depression between two rocky mounds, and turned the mare
up into the little crease and made his way with difficulty

up the side of the rocky hill. It was hard going, and he didn't want to push the mare too much. After he had gone a little over halfway, he pulled her up and then climbed down. He dropped her reins to the ground, knowing she would stand and wait. After that, he rummaged in his saddlebags and got out the two bundles of dynamite that contained four sticks. Holding one in each hand, he made his way with some difficulty toward the top of the hill. Longarm was guessing at his location but when finally, with a last labored effort, he cleared his head above the obstructing rocks, he was able to see down into the pasture. He was very close to where he had been turned over to Ernie and Charlie to be killed.

Longarm wasted very little time. He took one of the four-stick bundles and slipped down on the other side of the hill, moving carefully so as not to attract attention. Movement caught the eye more than shape or form. About a third of the way down the hillside, he found a cluster of rocks that looked like it would suit his needs. He slipped the four sticks in under the pile of rocks and with a trembling hand, crimped the blasting cap into the end of one of the sticks, leaving the fuse cord extending away from the dynamite. Then, still moving quickly but with caution, he proceeded on southerly for another fifty yards until he found another outcropping of rocks that he thought would suit his purpose. As quickly as he could, he buried the second bundle of dynamite in place, crimped those off with the blasting cap, and then reached into his pocket for a match.

With trembling fingers, he held the fuse cord in one hand and struck the match with the other. When the flame was going good, he held it to the fuse cord. It began to sputter. He immediately jumped up and moved as fast as he could to where he had left the first bundle of dynamite. There he struck another match and lit that fuse. He didn't wait to see if it was going good. He knew that with the first fuse burning, he only had a little time. All he wanted to do now was get over the hump of the hill and be protected. He could see his mare had backed partway down the hill until she was almost off it, her reins still hanging to the ground. She wouldn't run as long as those reins held her to the ground. As far as she was concerned, she was tied.

Longarm swung his head back around just as the first blast let go. The enormity of it startled even him. A huge cloud of rocks and dust and smoke rose in the air, and a boom like the end of the world shattered the stillness of the world. But that boom had no more than begun to die down when the second went off and the rocks and dirt and smoke again went flying in every direction. Longarm could see that in both cases the explosions had started small landslides. Rocks were still bounding down the hill from the first explosion. As he watched, he saw several riders approaching his way. He began to back down the hill as swiftly as he could. The explosion had startled the mare, but as steady as she was, she had recovered from the fright, and was now just standing away from the side of the mountain, looking up, trembling slightly.

It took Longarm another two or three minutes, but finally he was at the mare's side. He put a boot in the stirrup and swung aboard. Just south about a mile, right along the picket row of rocky hills, was a little grove of trees. He had noticed it earlier. He rode that way, riding just at the foot of the outcropping, but keeping far enough out so that his horse didn't step on a stray rock. In a matter of a few moments, he had the horse in among the little pine trees that grew where there was enough dirt to allow thirty or forty of them to take root. He rode into the grove, keeping the horse concealed, and then jumped down, pulling out his rifle from his boot as he did so. He started up the incline. At this point, the hill was not as rocky and it was much easier going. With labored breath, he dodged rocks and crevasses as he made his way to the top. He figured it would take some time for the riders to locate where the explosions had taken place and then to make their way to them. He expected them to be cautious. He had calculated that he would have the time to get to the firing spot well away from where he had set off the dynamite.

He reached the crest of the butte and went flat on his belly, slowly easing toward a line of sight to the prairie below. He took off his hat to better disguise his presence. He could see a half dozen to eight or ten riders coming. Most of them were headed from the south from where the big house and the outbuildings were located. He assumed that one of those outbuildings was a bunkhouse, maybe even more than one. A couple of other riders were coming from the east, across the pasture, and a couple more were coming from the north at the opening in the ring of hills. It was about what he'd expected. He pulled his Winchester up, cocking the hammer as he did, and sighted on the bunch of men riding from the ranch headquarters.

He had to wait, for they were too far away to get a good shot. As he watched, they neared, coming now to where they were only about six hundred yards away, then five hundred, then four hundred. He sighted on the lead rider and fired. Almost before the sound of the shot quit pounding in his ears, the rider went flipping off his horse and rolled over and over like a rag doll along the prairie. It caused the other riders to come to almost a complete stop. They were looking wildly around, not sure whether it was another explosion or a gunshot or just what it really was.

He took that time to lever another shell into his carbine and sight in on another rider. He fired, and that rider went over backward.

Now, they no longer hesitated in confusion. As one, the riders wheeled their horses and headed frantically back toward the south, the direction they had come from. Longarm got one more cartridge into the chamber and sighted on the back of the last man in line. He fired, and the rider slumped sideways in the saddle. For a second, it appeared that he would be able to hang on, but then the weight of his body pulled him off the side of his horse. He fell, landing on his head and shoulders and flipping up into the air, almost as if he was doing a handstand.

By now, the riders were out of sight. Longarm worked the lever of his carbine and looked to his left for the other four riders he had seen. One of them had veered toward the south, not aware, apparently, of the three men who had been shot. Longarm leveled his rifle, led the man a full yard, and then fired.

It was as if the rider had run into a clothesline, so quickly did he leave his horse. One second, the horse and rider were pounding over the prairie together. The next, the horse was going along and the rider was bouncing along on the ground. The other three riders pulled up and stopped. They glanced up toward the line of hills, looking to see where the fire was coming from. Longarm slipped slowly down below the top ridgeline and sat quietly. He was breathing more heavily than normal, but that was from the climb more than anything else.

He had just done something that was not in his nature to do. He had fired from ambush on men that he did not have a direct fight with, but the way he figured it, it didn't much matter. They worked for Vernon Ashton. And Vernon Ashton had decided to kill him or have him killed by such men as he had just shot. And if they were the kind of men who would kill another man just on the words of a man who paid them, then he felt no compunction and no guilt about ambushing them. They were his enemies plain and simple.

The curious part about it was that he could have understood if Ashton had suspected that he was a peace officer. That would have made sense. But Ashton had simply ordered him killed, probably just because he could. Longarm had presented himself as a horse trader, and Ashton had decided that he wasn't. So if indeed he had come there as an innocent horse trader, he would have still been killed if he hadn't been a United States deputy marshal, able to handle himself in a tight place.

The whole situation made him furious. He didn't reckon he had ever despised a man as much as he despised Vernon Ashton. It made him shake inside with anger, and if it was the last thing he ever did, he intended to wipe Vernon Ashton completely out. But he knew he couldn't do that as long as Ashton was surrounded by thirty or forty guns. Therefore, the only way to get to him was to get him naked—take off his clothes, take off his hired guns—and leave him standing there with only his own abilities to protect himself. Longarm would see how he liked that.

It had come a good dawn now, and Longarm still had a few chores left to do. He doubted that Ashton's gunhands would come so readily to the bait the next time, but he was going to make the bait much bigger in hopes that they would.

Aware now that he would have to proceed more carefully, Longarm made his way down to the little grove of pines. He caught up with his horse and rode further south along the base of the hill line. He glanced back toward town, but it was too far for him to see if there was any activity or if anyone had gotten curious about the explosions. He doubted that they had, though. As far away as Ashton's place was, the blast would have sounded almost identical to those that came twenty-four hours a day from the mines.

This time, Longarm rode a good long distance, almost two miles, perhaps a little further. He wanted to be much closer to Ashton's headquarters, but yet he didn't want to come directly even with it. He pulled his horse up and looked up the hill. This would be harder going. It was steeper and much more rocky. He wouldn't be able to use his horse to help him at all. He would have to climb the whole way in his high-heeled boots while carrying his rifle and the two bundles of dynamite. In the end, he put his saddlebags over his shoulder, took his rifle in his left hand, and started up the hill. He had taken time to reload his carbine, though he doubted that he would have a chance to use it.

It was hard going, and this part of the mountains was higher than the others had been. Now, he had to help himself along with his free hand, with the saddlebags flopping over his shoulder, trying to keep from banging his carbine against the rocks. It took him about fifteen minutes to reach the top, but when he did, he could see that he had picked a good spot. Very clear in the near foreground were the outbuildings. Two of them were long, low structures that he was willing to bet were bunkhouses. That was what he wanted to stir up. The other good thing was that there were plenty of rock heaps on the ranch side of the mountain.

Longarm knew he would have to work quick because it would be easy to spot him as he worked around the rocks.

He left his rifle on the off side and took the two bundles of dynamite, one containing six sticks and the one containing eight, and slipped over the crest of the little mountain. He worked his way about a third of the way down until he found some big boulders with some rocks the size of barrels. They looked to be just what he had in mind.

Now, he was going to do it a little more dangerously. He crimped the blasting cap into the end of the dynamite. This one had a six-foot cord. It would take three minutes for the fuse to burn. He put it in place, lit the fuse, and then hurried south along the mountain face, searching for a home for the eight-stick bundle. He didn't have to go but about a hundred yards. He found a small crevice in between a half-dozen rocks, and shoved the bundle in there. He crimped the blasting cap in place, and then lit the fuse. He turned and hurried as fast as he could to get to the crest. In a second, the bundle with six sticks was going to blast.

He had just made it over and onto the other side when there came a tremendous boom and roar. Longarm watched as a huge cloud of smoke and dust and dirt and rocks erupted from the other side of the mountain. When he was certain they were not going to rain down on him, he peeked over the edge. When he looked, he could see that some of the rocks were falling close enough to the outbuildings to draw the notice of the occupants. He saw one or two figures come to the door and look out. As quickly as he could he raced down to where he had left his rifle.

Just as he reached it, the second bundle went off, this blast sounding even louder than the other. As far away as he was, at least a hundred and fifty yards, he could still feel the thrust of the blast and the concussion as the air was blown apart. Now, as he looked down, he could see rocks hitting the buildings, including the two long, low structures he had taken to be bunkhouses. Half-a-dozen men had come out and looked up to see what had happened. These were men who had been asleep, who had not turned out for his first little attempt to get their attention. But they had come out now and were standing in the yard of the bunkhouse, staring up at the smoke and dust that were still rising.

They were too far away to make for anything but a lucky shot. But they were close together and there was a number of them. He levered a cartridge into the chamber and fired as quickly as he could, firing once, twice, three times. He fired six times until the hammer clicked on empty. He saw four men fall. He could not tell how badly they were hurt. As soon as the shells were spent, Longarm turned and hurried down the mountain as fast as he could. He had an idea that more work would be coming his way.

He got to his horse, but before he mounted, Longarm took a moment to reach into his saddlebags and take out some cartridges to reload. He leaned across the saddle, rammed the rifle home in its boot, and mounted up. He was moving a little more slowly than when he'd started. He did not recall ever running up and down so many hills before in all of his life. He also did not much like what he was doing, but he didn't see where he had any choice. It had been forced on him. A hand he hadn't cared to play had been dealt to him by a crooked dealer. Now he was going to make that dealer pay.

He turned the mare north, heading toward the break in the line of mountains. It was his guess that he had stirred up a hornet's nest and that the hornets were shortly going to be coming out of the hole in the nest. He was going to be there to greet them.

As he rode, he rapidly ran through his mind what damage

he possibly could have done. He knew of eight men, possibly ten, that he had finished off or seriously wounded that morning. Add to that the two from the day before, and he figured he had depleted Ashton of a quarter of his resources. He figured if he could get it down to about half, the men would begin to look at each other and wonder if they were being paid enough. It was one thing to lead the easy life and shoot strangers on Ashton's orders when you were in no danger yourself. They probably thought they were well paid, well fed, and well taken care of, but when men were dying around you, you had to wonder if you might possibly be next. Longarm didn't think they would view the job as such a plum.

At least, that was his hope. He hoped that he could discourage enough of them so that the rest would up and quit. He wanted Ashton on the ranch, all by himself in the big house with that good-looking Spanish woman. He didn't know about Early. He wasn't fooled by the man's cheerful face. He had marked the man down for a stone killer. There was no doubt in his mind that of the men he had seen, Early was the most dangerous.

But for the moment, the business at hand was all he needed thinking about. He got to the cleft in the hills and found a firing point some two hundred yards from the opening. He took his horse back around behind a rock outcropping and dropped the reins. She would have earned her oats before this day was out. Then he went back to the firing position he had selected. It was a good two hundred yards to the opening, but that was to his advantage. It was a long shot for him with a rifle on a rest, but it was going to be much longer for the men on horseback returning his fire. He didn't want to be too close and he didn't want to be too far. If they were coming, he felt that he was well placed.

Longarm got out a cigarillo, and lit it with one of the matches that he used to light the dynamite. He had to chuckle about the dynamite. It was damned handy stuff and would really cause a commotion. He had used it before, but only in single sticks that he had thrown. Never before had he used it the way you would use a cannon to blast rocks at somebody.

He smoked quietly, his eyes intent on the opening in the mountain. They had to come. They couldn't sit in there and let people blow them up and shoot them without coming out to see what was happening.

It was another five minutes before the first riders came walking their horses through the cleft. That was another advantage of the opening. A number of men couldn't come riding at top speed through it. It was strewn with rocks and it was narrow, so they had to take their time and they had to be careful.

Longarm was already sighted on where he wanted to fire. He waited until the fourth man in line filled his sights, and squeezed off a shot. The man went backward out of the saddle. Before he could get anywhere near the ground, Longarm had already levered another shell into the chamber and fired at the third man, the one in front of the one he had just shot. He too went flying off his horse, throwing his hands in the air.

There was a general commotion as the two men in front tried to turn back and those behind, uncertain what was happening, bulged forward. It was what Longarm had hoped would happen. Now, he fired at the backs of the two men trying to get away. One sagged forward over the neck of his horse, and the other grabbed at his shoulder and seemed to dismount more than fall. Fresh targets were presenting themselves, and he fired into the pack of men that were coming forward with the two shots he had left. He saw more confusion as one of the two men fell. His carbine was now empty and as quickly as he could, he grabbed up the cartridges he had laid out on the rock and rammed them home into the magazine. There was some shooting, but none of it seemed directed his way. They were just firing. Most of them were shooting handguns. Now there was just a mass of men in the opening, none of them going or coming. He fired six rapid shots into the bulk that he could see. He continued firing into the center of the confusion of men. He saw some bodies fall, but now they seemed to be retreating. Again, he reloaded. Longarm could feel the heat of the rifle barrel through his calloused left hand. As he threw his rifle up to his shoulder again, he could see that the opening was clearing out. He fired two more shots, but he doubted there were any results.

Longarm waited, watching. He could see men on the ground, some moving, some lying very still. A horse was down, and a few others were running around riderless, their bridles trailing on the ground. It was time, he thought, for him to make a quick departure before he could be seen or recognized or even located. He didn't think any of them had known where the fire had come from. Bending low, he raced around the outcrop to where his mare was waiting. Holding his rifle in his right hand, he stuck a boot in the stirrup and swung aboard. Then he sat off riding the mare at a high lope heading toward the north, circling around the foothills of the mountains. He kept going that way until the rise and fall of the land would hide him from view of the entrance to Ashton's place.

When he was certain he couldn't be seen, he turned to the northwest, toward town. He wanted to come into town from an angle where it would look like he hadn't been anywhere near Ashton's place. As he rode, he kept circling further and further to the west to circle around and come in from the west. Finally, he pulled the mare down to a trot, and then to a slow walk, and then let her amble her way into the back side of town. He directed her to the livery stable and then stopped her. She was a little fatigued. She'd had some pretty good runs that morning. He dismounted and handed the reins to the stable boy, along with a quarter. He said, "Rub her down, sonny. Take right good care of her. She's been hard at work."

Longarm turned and walked around the hotel, stepped up on the porch, went through the front door, and then went through the dining room. His stomach was telling him it was well past time for breakfast. The clock on the wall said it was ten minutes after eight, and that was mighty late.

As he crossed the lobby, he saw Finley coming down the stairs. He stopped until the rancher or land broker, or whatever he was, could reach the ground floor and come up to him. "Well, good morning, Mr. Finley," he said. "I'm just now going in for breakfast. Would you care for coffee?"

Finley cocked his head. "Just going in for breakfast? My heavens, Mr. Long. You keep odd hours for a man used to trading livestock. I thought you boys tried to make most of your deals before the sun got up." He laughed slightly. "So you couldn't see the merchandise so good."

Longarm said, "Well, as it happens, that is exactly what I've been doing. Actually, I've just been looking some of the country over to see how it might fare as a place to hold some horses. I need some sort of intermediate pastureland since I am doing more business to the south and it's a good long run from Oregon."

"Didn't I see you ride out east of here?"

Longarm let a beat pass before he answered. He slowly shook his head. "No, I've been all around, but I don't think I've been to the east that I know of, been looking more to the west. That's mainly mining country to the east, isn't it?"

"Yeah, and that's where Ashton's place is."

Longarm shook his head again. "No, I wouldn't know anything about Mr. Ashton. On your advice, I completely forgot about him."

Finley nodded. "Well, I've got to get about the day. I'd like to get finished up here and get on back home."

Longarm said, "Did you ever say where that was?"

"What?"

"Home."

"No, I guess I didn't. Well, you take it easy, Mr. Long." Then he turned and was gone out the front door of the hotel.

Longarm watched him thoughtfully for a moment before walking into the dining room and sitting down tiredly. He'd had a big morning. When the waiter came over, he ordered coffee and ham and eggs and flapjacks. He said, "And I wish you'd put some whiskey in my coffee."

The waiter said, "I reckon we can do that, sir."

Longarm nodded. "Much obliged."

Chapter 5

About ten o'clock that morning, the town was abuzz. Sometime before, two men riding hard had come in to fetch the doctor out to Vernon Ashton's headquarters. They had rushed him and pushed him and practically shoved him on his horse. Fortunately, the doctor was a young man and able to stand the hard ride they apparently were going to put him through. During the time he was gone, the town did nothing but talk about it.

The two men who had come in were closemouthed. They had given no indication of the trouble. Indeed, they had said not a word to anyone who had questioned them about their need for the doctor. They wouldn't say if Ashton was sick, or if any of the hands were sick, or if any of the ladies who lived out there were sick. They had refused any news of any kind.

It wasn't until a little after one o'clock in the afternoon that the doctor returned. He came back looking haggard, with blood on his shirt and on his pants. You could see from the way he rode his horse into the livery stable and dismounted that he'd had a lively time of it. He took his doctor's bag and then walked down the sidewalk, while everyone stopped and stared at him, and then went into his office.

For quite a while, no information could be learned. The doctor had a clerk, a young man named Bill, who received his visitors and took their payments if they offered them. At first, Bill wouldn't talk. Not a word could be gotten out of him, but finally the doctor closed his office and went home. Bill went into the Elite Saloon, and was immediately surrounded by the curious. He didn't know much, but after a few drinks, he was willing to tell what he did know. He said that the doctor had treated four gunshot wounds, that three of them were very serious, and that the men might not live. The one not so serious had resulted in a broken arm, and that man would be all right. The doctor didn't know if a fight had broken out amongst the men themselves, or if there had been an attack of some kind, or just what had happened. Bill said that the doctor had been taken straight into a bunkhouse, and that he had worked on the men on a table in there, and that he had been paid and that was all Bill knew.

Of course, they wanted to know where the other men had been shot, and if there had been other men lying around that might have been shot but were past the doctor's help. Bill couldn't answer any of that. They wondered how much the doctor had gotten paid. Bill did know that, but he thought he ought not say. And he didn't until he had been bought two more drinks. After that, he said with some amazement that the doctor had received a hundred dollars for making the trip and for his doctoring.

It was all anyone could talk about. Ashton was always a mystery and always a fund of curiosity. Now this had happened, and it was anybody's guess what it meant. It scared some people that it might mean that Ashton could be in trouble to the point that he might leave the area. That put a fright into any number of merchants. One was heard to say that if anybody had attacked Vernon Ashton and had shot up his men, that man ought to be strung up. And he, by golly, would be the one to put the rope around the neck of any party that would give such a fine man as Vernon Ashton a hard time. The owner of the saloon and casino was seen walking around, staring several men in the face. It was as if he was making certain that they had not been a part of such mischief. It was well known that the trade from the Ashton ranch made up a good part of his business.

Listening to it all in snatches and bits, and from what he could overhear without making himself conspicuous, Longarm could see why Finley had warned him that the town was solidly behind the reclusive man in the castle. Of course, the town didn't know that all that business he was giving them was paid for with counterfeit twenty-dollar bills, probably taken out in saddlebags. That was one good thing about paper money. You didn't need a wagon team to haul it as you did with gold, and you could carry a great amount stuffed into somebody's saddlebags or a carpetbag.

Standing out in the street, casually listening to the conversation going on, Longarm noticed Finley looking his way. He gave the man a friendly wave and sauntered toward him. "Well, wonder what the hell happened out at Ashton's?" Longarm said.

Finley fixed him with a pair of hard blue eyes. "I reckon you'd know as well as I would."

The tone of his voice startled Longarm. "Why would that be?" he asked. "Hell, I'm just a stranger. I don't know a damned thing."

"Well, where were you this morning when all this was happening?"

Longarm drew his head back. "Look here, Finley. I've done told you that. I'm schooling a gelding that needed some work, and I rode out in the exact opposite direction. Ask them down at the livery stable which direction they saw me coming from; don't take my word for it. What business is it of yours anyway? Do you work for Ashton?"

Finley shook his head. "No, but what affects this town could affect me, and what affects Ashton affects this town. Do you follow my way of thinking?"

Longarm said, "I follow it, though I can't say I much care for it."

He turned and walked away, considerably nettled. Finley had been the only man in the town that he had felt like being friendly with, and now Finley was turning out to be the biggest busybody. Of course, the man was right. Longarm had been out early, and he had been doing some work at about the time the dynamite had exploded and people were getting shot. But still, Finley shouldn't be drawing such quick conclusions.

Longarm went back to his room, poured himself a glass of the Maryland whiskey, and sat down on the bed with the whiskey and a cigarillo to have a think. The best he could figure, including the shooting at the notch in the wall, he had taken out about fifteen of Ashton's men. Maybe he hadn't killed fifteen, but he reckoned he had let some light through at least that many. He wondered what the rest of them were thinking. He had heard some of the townspeople say that the two men who had come in to get the doctor were as mad as wet setting hens, and that it would be a smart idea for people to stay clear of the ranch for the time being because all the riders had orders to shoot first and then find out who they shot later. None of the townspeople seemed willing to debate the point. It made Longarm think.

His plan had been to go ahead and take his second step that very next morning at around two o'clock, but now he wasn't sure. He felt certain they would be patrolling the perimeters, especially the side of the pasture where he had set off the dynamite initially. It might be to his advantage to give them twenty-four hours to think the matter over.

He hated the idea, however, mainly because he wanted to finish the job and get the hell out of Silverton. It was a tiresome place to stay. There wasn't much to do except gamble in the cheap casino, where only a jughead would risk his money at the house odds. You might as well just send it over rather than bother to play. That left poker, and the only decent game he had found had been the one he had played with Finley that first night. Well, he guessed he could always try at Ashton's again, but it probably was wisest to wait twenty-four hours, even though he was very anxious not only to leave, but also to lay his hands on Vernon Ashton. Thoughts also flashed through his mind about the Spanish-looking woman he had seen on the stair landing. She was a right comely young lady and very well built, especially in the breast and hip area. He was a breast man for certain. He wasn't particular as to size, but he did like them firm and he did like them to have big nipples. She looked like the kind to have big rosettes and big nipples.

Those thoughts made him smile to himself. Here he was, a long way from any female comfort, and he knew better than to be thinking about breasts and nipples. There was certainly no help in this town except for whores. He had never paid a whore in his life, and didn't reckon he'd ever start. Of course, he had never charged one either. He reckoned they were all square.

The day dragged on. He ate lunch, and then spent some

93

time in his room, resting and drawing a map on paper of Ashton's layout. He had fixed it in his mind, but he wanted to make sure he knew what outbuilding was where, what outbuilding was likely to contain men, and just how far it was to the house, the best estimate he could make.

Once he drew it out on the paper he had gotten at the desk, he looked at it a long time until he had committed it to memory. He struck a match and then burned the paper, dropping it into a wastebasket. Later in the afternoon, he took his saddlebags and went over to the hardware store. He picked up the second box of dynamite he had already paid for, only this time instead of carrying it on his shoulders, he got the hardware store owner to open the box and put the dynamite and blasting caps and some fuse cord into his saddlebags. It nearly filled them up, and made a little bit of a load as he walked back to the livery stable with the saddlebags over his shoulder. He figured it would be safer, less conspicuous, and less likely to be seen there in the livery stable in the stall of the mare. He put it up at her head, took some spare hay, and covered the saddlebags with that. Now, at least, when he left the hotel to go on his next assignment, he wouldn't be carrying the dynamite where people might notice. This way, all he would have to do was go to the livery stable, saddle up his horse, and then tie the saddlebags in place, and he would be in business.

He had already begun to realize that there were too many busybodies around town who stood ready to nose into any business that might seem, in any way, connected with what had happened to Vernon Ashton and his men. So far as that went, he figured they hadn't seen anything yet. He intended to give Ashton's hired hands a little more of the same. Nobody would be fool enough to keep a job, even if they were paying him a hundred dollars a month, if there was an excellent chance that he was going to be killed the next day.

He ended up that night at the saloon, and sat in a poker game. He had been playing about an hour and a half when Finley came in. A chair happened to come open about that time, and Finley took it. He gave Longarm a friendly nod as he sat down, and Longarm returned it.

Finley said, "Well, how are the cards running this evening, Mr. Long?"

"Just middling," Longarm said. "Just middling."

"Well, you have enough chips stacked up in front of you. I figured you must be making it warm for these other fellows."

"These ain't exactly sheep. In fact, you might say that there are more wolves in here than there are sheep. Now, I think we just got one more."

Finley gave a lighthearted chuckle. He said, "Oh, Mr. Long. I think we know who wears the long teeth."

They played without anything particularly interesting happening for the next several hands. Then, in a hand of five-card draw, Longarm went into the discard with three queens. He opened for ten dollars. Two of the other players and Finley called him. Longarm threw away two cards and took two. The two cards he took turned out to be a pair of nines. He had a full house, queens over nines, a very strong hand.

Finley sweated his cards in one at a time, looking at them carefully. He glanced across at Longarm and said, "Opener's bet."

Longarm said to the dealer, "How many cards did Mr. Finley take?"

"He took one."

Longarm nodded. "Drawing for a full house, Mr. Finley?"

"Well, I don't think a straight is going to be good enough to beat you, so I was trying for a full house, yes. Of course, this is poker and you're supposed to tell the truth at all times."

"Oh, yes," Longarm said. He counted out fifty dollars and made the bet. The first man to his left dropped out. Finley called the fifty dollars and raised it fifty. That made it a hundred dollars to the fourth player. He threw his hand in as fast as he could.

The man said, "Hell, I've got a child's hand. What are you boys playing at?"

Longarm thought about it for a moment. Then he called Finley's fifty and raised him back another hundred. A hush fell over the table. This was serious poker. This was poker designed for other places. It didn't get played in this saloon, in this casino. It was high-stakes poker.

Finley looked at his cards for a long time, and then at the pile of money in front of him. He said, almost as if he were speaking to no one, "You know, you can buy a pretty good saddle horse for a hundred dollars. You ought to know that, you being a horse trader, Mr. Long."

"Mr. Finley, right now, I am not a horse trader. Right now, I am a poker player with three of a kind, hoping you don't have that flush or straight."

"Oh, I've got that flush or straight. I'm just hoping you ain't full or made four of a kind."

"Well, if I had a flush or straight and I was in your shoes, I'd raise me back a hundred."

Finley laughed, but without much humor. "That's the difference in us, Mr. Long. You ain't in my shoes and I ain't in yours. I'll just call."

Longarm showed his full house. Finley nodded and said, "That's good." Then, without showing his cards, he threw them in the discard pile and stood up. "I reckon I've had about all the cards I can stand for one evening."

Without another word, Finley gathered up his money and walked out of the saloon, not even bothering to stop for a drink. Longarm watched him as he left. There was something about Finley that was bothering him, and he couldn't place it. He was almost certain that he had some connection with Ashton and didn't want anyone to know. Perhaps he was Ashton's spy to see what law might be coming into the town of Silverton. Maybe he was lookout. Maybe his job was to spot strangers and find out their business and relay that information to Ashton. Maybe that was what had given Longarm away.

Longarm played on for about another hour, and then stretched and got up and left the game. He was a solid two hundred dollars ahead, and he figured that was enough. He had lost a few hands at the last just to sweeten up the local players, doing it deliberately and allowing himself to be caught bluffing. It always made everyone feel better if the big winner lost a little something just before he walked away.

To make things even better, he stopped by the bar on his way, bought a bottle of whiskey, and had it sent to the table. He was out the door before they could even shout their thanks.

It was coming close to midnight by the look of the moon, and he walked slowly back to the hotel. The moon was coming full. It was going to be a good one to work by if he could get his business in order while it was still up. He went to his room and had a couple of drinks of Maryland whiskey before turning in and sleeping the sleep of the just.

He woke early, and was ready for breakfast by six-thirty. Strangely enough, even though he dawdled, Finley did not come in. There were other cafes in town, and he supposed the man might have chosen another, but it did seem odd.

He lazed around the rest of the day. He took the bay gelding out for some exercise and some schooling. The bay was not four years old, and not as smart as he ought to be. He was also still a little spooky. Longarm showed him his shadow every now and then just to see if he would jump. He spooked at some sagebrush that rustled, and then nearly turned inside out when a rabbit suddenly jumped up out of the prairie in front of them. For a few seconds, Longarm was hard pressed to stay on the back of the horse. Just so the gelding wouldn't forget what his job was, Longarm gave him a good long ten-mile ride, circling far out to the north and the west and then coming back into town.

He was late for lunch at the hotel, and the dining room was closed by the time he'd put the gelding up and come in and cleaned up. There was a free lunch at the saloon, but a man had to be pretty damned hungry to take part in that. He finally found a chili place run by a Mexican and his wife. He sat there eating chili with corn tortillas and drinking cold beer. It might have been the best meal he'd had since he'd been in town. But they didn't serve breakfast, so this hadn't been the place where Finley had taken his morning meal. Longarm shut down that line of thought. He was starting to see buggers under the bed like some old maid. Ninety-nine chances out of a hundred, or even more than that, Finley was exactly what he said he was, a man who just didn't want to see any trouble come to the mountain valley. Longarm couldn't blame him. If he was going to be in a peaceful business, he wouldn't want to see explosions and gunfights and gunshot victims.

Longarm hung around the saloon that afternoon. He had a reason, and at about four o'clock, he was not surprised to see the two hard, young strangers with their guns set up like they knew how to use them standing at the bar looking bitter and taking straight shots of whiskey without bothering to sip at it.

No one was going near them. In fact, the other patrons were keeping a respectful distance. Longarm asked one man who they might be, and the man whispered back that they were riders for Vernon Ashton and that it looked like they were clearing out. It seemed like they were mad as hornets, the man said.

Longarm ambled forward like a man with nothing much on his mind, and got up next to the bar close to the two men. He ordered a bottle of the best from the bartender and poured himself out a shot. The two men scarcely glanced at him. He offered the bottle down to them. He said, ''Care for a drink, boys?'' Their glasses were both empty, and they hadn't had time to refill them.

They both glared at him, but one of them made a slight condescending nod with his head. Longarm slopped whiskey into both of their shot glasses, and then held his own up and said, ''Well, here's to luck.''

The one closest to him said, ''Yeah. Bad luck. Sonofabitch. Worst damned luck I've ever seen.''

They all drank the whiskey straight down, and Longarm was quick with the bottle again.

This time, he said, ''You boys look a little down and out. Something troubling you?''

The one closest to him turned his head and spat tobacco juice on the floor. He said, ''Hell, what ain't the matter? That sonofabitch. We gave him good work. We protected him, we risked our lives, and we ask the sonofabitch to pull in the horns a little bit, and the bastard don't want to do the right thing.''

The man on the other side of him said, "Yeah, that's about the size of it. We're pulling stakes and getting the hell out of here. Two good years we wasted here. To hell with him."

Longarm said carefully, "You would be talking about Mr. Ashton?"

The tobacco chewer spat again. He said, "Hell, no. We're talking about Mr. Early. He's the boss. We wanted to concentrate up while this little trouble was going on, but he wanted everybody to keep riding patrols like we have been doing. Hell, that's just damned foolishness. We wanted to rout out whoever this troublemaker was. We wanted to come into town in a bunch and find out who was causing the trouble. But he said no, he weren't for it. Well, the hell with him. The others out there feels the same as we do, but they just haven't moved yet."

Longarm thought, but didn't say, that the fact that they might be getting killed fairly quickly was also a reason to leave. But if they wanted to believe they were leaving because they didn't agree with the boss, that was all right with him. He poised the bottle over their glasses and poured them full again. He said, "Can't blame you. Damn bosses, they don't ever see the workingman's side of it, do they?"

By now, Longarm's approach had emboldened the rest of the men in the saloon, and they came crowding up to the bar to talk to the two riders and to buy drinks and ask questions. Longarm slipped out as easily as he could.

The day wore on. The riders hadn't told him anything that he hadn't expected to hear. He was just surprised that only two had quit. He couldn't make a real count, but it seemed to him that he was close to halving Ashton's force. If it hadn't been for that damned Early, probably more would have left. Longarm was under no illusions that if he ever rode onto that place as a marshal with a six-gun in his hand, it would be Early that he would have to fight and that he would have to be the most wary of.

Longarm ate supper in the dining room of the hotel, and then went back to his room and played solitaire with an old deck of cards he had been carrying around a while. He didn't think he would go to the poker game that night because of the hour in which he was leaving. He had thought to catch a couple hours sleep, but about ten o'clock, he realized that would be impossible. He put his cards away and went over to the saloon.

Once again, Finley was not among those playing cards. Nor was he at the bar nor was he sitting in the casino area. Longarm was a little surprised, but then again, he almost hadn't come himself. Maybe the man was back in his room, figuring his business or writing a letter home. Hell, it was none of Longarm's business. None, except that he had a sinking suspicion about the man.

He sat in on a game without much enthusiasm, and played about the same way. At the end of an hour and a half, he'd lost about thirty dollars, and he decided that that was enough to donate to such poor poker players. He couldn't draw any cards. The rule was that the best hand won unless you could run somebody out, and they weren't playing with enough money to successfully run a bluff.

He didn't bother with a drink on the way out. He had his Maryland whiskey, and he preferred that to the bar stuff. Besides, when he stepped outside, he knew it wouldn't be long before he would be leaving. The moon was high in the sky, and he reckoned it was a little before midnight. It was good and full, a big gold orb just hanging up in a black, cloudless sky. It threw a good shooter's light. Of course, that cut both ways. It would make it easier for him to see, but it would also make it easier for him to be seen.

He went back to his room and had a couple of cigarillos and a drink or two of his whiskey. He thought over his plan, looking for holes in it. It was a simple straightforward piece of business that would either work or it wouldn't. That was all it amounted to.

At one o'clock, he stood up, checked the ammunition in his rifle, and made sure he had rifle ammunition in his shirt pockets and pistol ammunition in both pants pockets. He turned and walked out the door, heading for the livery stable. The moon was still up, still full, and it was still throwing a lot of light. By the time it went down, he ought to know something.

Chapter 6

About 2:30, he had all in readiness. He had ridden the mare, loaded down with the forty sticks of dynamite, twenty in each side of the bag. He had brought along tape, blasting caps, and fuse. He made his way up the side of the mountain, having a hard time of it with the dynamite and his rifle. He had to make two trips, but he had been careful not to highlight himself by raising his head above the crest of the hill. He had picked a point even further south than before, where he was almost an equal distance between the house and the two bunkhouses. The bunkhouses were narrow and ran side by side away from him. They were a little closer to the side of the hills than the big house was. There were other outbuildings, but he wasn't concerned with them.

Now, working as quietly as he could, he taped twenty of the dynamite sticks together. He couldn't do it in one bundle at one time. He had to tape them five at a time, and then put four bundles of five together and tape them. After that, he rammed home a blasting cap with six feet of fuse in it. He had already picked out his place. There was a large pile of rocks and boulders about halfway down the slope. It was exactly what he had in mind. It should give him a cannonade of large proportions. He slipped down the side of the small mountain and buried his dynamite in place. Next, he went back up and worked the rest of the dynamite into a similar bundle. This time, he put a two-foot cord on the bundle. That was enough for only one minute. Not a lot to play with.

As he was slipping down the mountain, groping his way, not so much from the darkness but from the uncertain footing, he chanced to see a dark shadow out of the corner of his eye, down on the ground, perhaps fifty yards from the base of the hill. He froze, and tried to make himself look like a rock. It was a rider. Longarm could see him sitting his horse, staring up, but couldn't do anything. For a second, he was fearful the man would raise the alarm. But just then, the rider turned his horse in the direction of the big house and started riding, taking his horse in a slow trot.

The moment the rider's back was to him, Longarm wasted no time. He immediately came out with a match and lit the fuse. As he did so, he stood up and started to turn. It was at that instant that the man riding the horse must have seen the flame from his match, or else the sparkle of the fuse, for he immediately wheeled his horse around and started riding hard back toward where Longarm was standing. Longarm turned. Knowing he could not stay there with that short fuse, he started to run to the other bundle of dynamite. He heard a shot ring out, and heard it strike rock and go singing off. He stopped, and fell down by the rock pile where he had buried the rest of the dynamite. He could see the man levering his rifle for another shot, but he knew the man couldn't see him where Longarm was hidden. He struck another match and then lit the fuse, and made a quick scrambling run to the crest of the hill and fell over. As he did, he heard another rifle bullet sing through the air, and heard the crack of the man's carbine.

In that same second, the first bundle of dynamite went off and the blast almost knocked Longarm down. The blast was enough to deafen him. He stood in awe as he saw the billows of rocks and dirt and debris go flying straight toward the bunkhouses and toward the ranch. The man who had been firing at him was standing almost directly in the way. Even on a fast horse, he'd never have a chance.

Longarm stood up and watched, smelling the cordite in the air, as big rocks, some as big as a saddle, plummeted down on the two bunkhouses. He could see holes appearing in the roofs of the two buildings. Strangely enough, no one came running out. He thought he knew why. The last time they came out, they had been fired on. Some of the smaller rocks had hit the house. He saw some break a window. It made him feel good. He half whispered, "How do you like them apples, Mr. Ashton."

He had almost forgotten about the second blast, and was standing right straight behind it on the crest of the mountain. When it went, it caused him to stagger backward. The wind of the concussion wave hit him and almost knocked him down. He did not notice the noise so much this time, as he had almost been deafened by the first blast.

The second was practically a duplicate of the first, except the rocks seemed to go further because they were smaller. Again, he could see holes appearing in the walls and the roofs and the windows. He had his carbine ready to fire on anyone who came out. No one appeared. He didn't really think anyone was going to appear until the next day. Off in the distance, he could see a few riders going back and forth, but they didn't seem to be in any rush to charge to the rescue of the ranch headquarters. It made Longarm smile.

He took his rifle and went down the hill to where his horse was tied. He mounted up and then rode toward the cleft in the rocks, the exit from the ranch. He took his place behind the same boulder he had been behind the last time. If they wanted to come out, he was willing to meet them halfway. In fact, if they came out as a peace party, he would even meet them that way. He settled down to wait.

Less time passed than he would have guessed. All of a sudden, out of the pitch blackness of the hole in the side of the mountain came a loud "Hello!" It was repeated. "Hello! Hello out there!"

Longarm turned his head a little so that the direction of his voice wouldn't be so easy to place. He said, "I hear you. Go ahead."

The voice said, "I don't know who you be, but we've had enough. There's me and six others who want to come out and go our way. We ain't got no guns in our hands and we don't want no trouble. We don't know what your quarrel is with this here ranch, but we are quitting it. We don't work here no more. We don't work no more for Mr. Ashton. We don't work for Mr. Early no more. We'd just as soon not be shot down. Play square with us. Tell us what your plans are."

Longarm peered over the top of the boulder he was sequestered behind. He said, "If you're telling the truth, you've got nothing to fear. If you're not, you're going to get a .44 cartridge in the middle of your forehead. I'll make you a third eye."

"We are telling the truth. We are quitting this game, throwing our hands in. Now, what do we do?"

Longarm said as he squinted over the sights of his rifle,

"Come out one at a time, slow, and bear sharp to the south."

"You want our hands in the air or what?"

"Just put your hands on your saddle horns. You might fall off if you have your hands in the air. You never can tell when a horse will spook with a high moon like we have tonight."

"A couple of us are hurt from some of those damned rocks that got rained down on us. We need to get into town and see the doctor."

Longarm said, "I'm telling you, ride due south. If you figure seeing the doctor is worth your life, then you go ahead. But I'll be there and I'll turn you back."

He could hear muffled voices. The voice of the spokesman said, "All right. Have it your way. We can find a doctor on down the road. You mean, you don't want us going into Silverton at all. Is that it?"

"That's the ticket," Longarm said. "You stay clear of Silverton. For the time being, I don't want them knowing what's up."

"Do you mind telling us what your business is, mister?"

Longarm said, "It ain't none of yours. Now, do you want out of there or not? I'm going to start counting, and if you ain't moving by the time I get to one, I'm going to start firing into that hole."

The man said hurriedly, "We are coming. Hold on!"

The next thing Longarm could see was a horseman exiting the cleft, bearing sharply to his left, and riding at a slow trot, heading down toward the mining camps, which were fifteen to twenty miles away.

Another man came out, and then another and then another, until seven riders had left the confines of the ranch.

Longarm called to the last two, "Hold up, you two. Hold up."

They dragged their horses in reluctantly. The tail man said, "Hell, mister. I'm one of the ones that are hurt. A rock hit me on the shoulder and liked to cave it in. I wish you'd let me go on and get some help."

"Tell me the truth and you can go quick as you want to. Who is left on that ranch?"

The other man with him spoke up. He said, "We don't rightly know. There was five going to try and get out the southeast end of the place, but it's a rough way to go. You've got to damned near lead your horses through some tough, rough terrain. It's rocky as hell, but they were going to try it."

"What about Early?"

The hurt man said, "Oh, he's still there. I reckon he's in the big house with Mr. Ashton and the women."

Longarm's ears perked up. He said, "Women? How many women?"

"Well, there's Ashton's sweetheart, if that's what she is, or his whore, whichever one you want to call it. And then there's her aunt or her mother or her chaperone or whatever. Then there's a couple of maids."

"You're telling me that all there is in there is Early and Ashton."

The hurt man said, "I wouldn't take that any too lightly, neighbor. Early ain't no bad hand. If I were you, mister, I wouldn't let that friendly smile he gets on his face fool you none. Inside, he's the very devil. I wouldn't be in no rush to go slinging on in there. I don't know what your business is, and I don't know why you've gone through so much trouble to run us out. You've done a good job at that. But you might find the going a little rough from here on in."

Longarm said, "Do you think those five got out?"

The man shrugged. "I couldn't say, mister. I reckon they did, or else they'd be down here trying to get out. I know one thing. They are leaving one way or the other."

Longarm eased the hammer down on his rifle. He said, "Ride on. Sorry about your shoulder, but that's what comes from working for the wrong man."

The hurt man said, "Well, you better hope that you don't get a chance to say that about yourself. Let's go, Charlie."

The men rode on, catching up with the rest, headed away from Silverton, due south toward the mining camps. Longarm stood up slowly and walked over and shoved his rifle into the boot. It was just about time to go and settle matters with Ashton. He hoped the man would not have destroyed any evidence. His job, after all, was to get the plates or paper or whatever they called it that the man used to make counterfeit bills. That was what he was going to do.

Chapter 7

He waited for a short time. The moon was heading down now, going out of sight behind the higher peaks of the mountains. Soon, it would be at the darkest part of the night. He wanted the cover of that darkness to make his approach to Ashton's castle. There might have been only two men left there, but either one of them could accidentally put a bullet through Longarm's middle. He was all too aware of that.

He sat the mare just inside the cleft in the mountain with the clear prairie before him, watching the moon, letting it get darker and darker. When he judged it to be around four o'clock in the morning, he nudged the mare and began slowly making his way toward Ashton's headquarters, all the while sweeping his eyes across the prairie, looking for any riders that might have forgotten to leave.

He rode up as close to the little line of hills as he could, hoping to blend in with the dark rock. He couldn't see a thing stirring, and he hoped that it would continue that way. He had no real plan except to get in the main headquarters, get Ashton by the collar, and see if he could talk with a .44-caliber revolver barrel in his mouth. After he got the plates and the cash and the paper or whatever, he figured he could pay the young *señorita* some attention and then whomp them all up, wrap them up in a box, tie them up with a ribbon, and take them back to Billy Vail.

It was easy to tell where he had set off his explosions, for the ground was thick with rocks, some as big as baseballs and some nearly as big as woodstoves. He was still a good ways from the outbuildings and the headquarters, but he was in no hurry. He wanted to get there right before dawn, when it was as black as it was going to get. That old saying, "It's always darkest just before dawn," was one that he hoped would prove true this morning. It wasn't always the case, depending on the moon up.

The mare was behaving herself very well. She had been a good using animal on this trip. He figured there ought to be some way he could charge the government for her use as well as for her groceries and her transportation. He would figure out a way to put it on his expense voucher. Billy Vail would raise hell but in the end, he would pay for it. Especially if Longarm was successful on his errand to capture the man who was making twenty-dollar gold certificates.

Longarm moved the pace up a little as the moon finally began to fade from the sky. Now, he was nearing the place where he had set off the first of the twenty-stick explosions. The bunkhouses were just ahead and to his left. He veered over to get away from the big piles of rubble that the large amounts of dynamite had blasted out of the hills. It looked like some giant hand had come along and swept rocks down onto the grassy prairie. It seemed a waste to Longarm to see all that good land going to waste—not a cow in sight. Now and again, he could see a loose horse, riderless, out grazing. He wondered about the five men who had been trying to get out the south end. He didn't know how they would act, but to be ready, he eased his rifle out of the boot and continued on, keeping watch and being careful to guide his horse through the debris of the explosion.

He didn't expect to have to fight the five men. He rather expected that they'd had enough trouble and like the others, were pretty well beaten down. He kept an eye on the moon, waiting for its last rays to fade. He still had to be careful with his horse, because now he was in the area where his big bomb had exploded and there were some good-sized rocks in his path. He steered his horse left toward the dim outline of the two bunkhouses. It came to his mind that he should dismount fairly soon and proceed ahead on foot. A man was a good deal easier to see on a horse.

Longarm came even with the bunkhouses. They were still dark, and there was not a sound. He pulled the mare up to listen. Again, there was nothing. He decided, with the main house only about a quarter of a mile further on, that it was time for him to go ahead on foot. He hated to walk in his high-heeled boots, but it was better than getting shot out of the saddle.

The moon had dropped down until it had finally disappeared behind the last crag of mountains. There was a faint afterglow in the sky, but the darkness was almost as complete as it would get. Longarm eased his leg over the back of the saddle, hearing the creak of the leather in the quiet night. He continued on until he dismounted. He dropped the reins of the mare, and then took a few steps forward and holding his rifle at the ready, peered carefully into the dark gloom of the night that lay ahead of him. There was no sign of light anywhere, not even in the big house.

He stepped out, moving slowly but carefully. He passed

113

the first of the bunkhouses, and then the second. There was a space, and then beyond that was a small barn. There was a bigger one behind that. He was looking for movement. He saw none. He kept walking slowly, carefully, ever alert, the rifle ready in his hands. It was ready to fire from the hip or throw to his shoulder. Ahead now were nothing but a small stone house and then the big castlelike structure of Ashton's. He walked toward the small stone house, made to seem small only in comparison to the size of Ashton's place. He wondered if the one-story house, if it was that, was where they actually did the counterfeiting, where the plates and the paper and whatnot were stored. It didn't seem to have any windows in it that he could see, though he wasn't close enough in the dark to be able to really tell. There could have been windows that were curtained over that he wasn't able to see. He directed his steps, turning to his left and heading toward the smaller house. It was all brick, no wooden framework on it as there was on Ashton's house.

Not a light showed from the building. He doubted there was anyone there. Likely, it had been the home of one of the foreman. Maybe it still was. Maybe that foreman was still in there. If that was the case, Longarm couldn't afford to pass the place and have it to his back when he was trying to enter Ashton's house.

He stopped for a moment to reach around and adjust his gun belt. When he dismounted, he had taken the trouble to take out his spare revolver and stick it in the back waistline of his pants. It was uncomfortable and awkward and weighed down on his gun belt, but though a spare gun was something you might never need, if you did, you might need it awful bad. You never knew when you might get into a shooting fix where the six you were carrying in your revolver was one bullet too short. Then you really wanted that second gun. But a .44-caliber revolver was a heavy piece of business, and he had to get it resettled before he could move along.

Longarm looked at the small building, and then took a few steps to the low stone porch. There was no sign of activity inside, but he was going to have to open the door and make an examination before he could risk going on. He'd bypassed the bunkhouses, for it was clear they were deserted. He couldn't take the time to examine every outbuilding, but this little house stood so close to the castle, it would be almost at his back when he was trying to gain entry.

He stepped up on the porch, and then moved swiftly across and felt the door handle. It turned easily in his hand. It wasn't locked. He pushed it open and then stepped back out of the way, clear of the opening. Nothing happened. He stood still, trying to stifle the sound of his own breathing. After a moment, he peeked around the door frame to see what he could of the inside.

It was very difficult to see anything, for it was darker inside than it was on the outside. Stooping a little, holding the rifle in front of him, he stepped into the front part of the building. After a moment, his eyes adjusted and he could see that there were very few windows, and those that were there were covered with curtains of some kind. He moved along, taking each step carefully, sliding his boot across the floor with as little disturbance as he could manage.

He spent a full quarter of an hour in the place, and the best he could figure was that if someone lived there, they did so in only one room. That was the only place where he found a bed and a chest of drawers and some clothes in a closet. The other room seemed vacant, bare. He couldn't understand why anyone would build such a structure and only use one room. But it was certain that he wasn't going to find the answer while standing there in the dark with a rifle pointed at nothing.

He went back out through the door, stepping into the night. It seemed almost light after the gloom of the interior of the stone building. Now, he began to walk toward Ashton's castle. He was coming up on the side. He could see that there was a long, low stone wall that surrounded the immediate property, at least on his side of the house. If he recollected correctly from his first visit, he had passed through sort of an opening. The wall wasn't very tall, perhaps three feet or three and a half. It wouldn't keep anybody out.

Longarm walked slowly toward the house, studying its every aspect, wondering how he was going to get in without shooting out a lock. He was about ten yards from the low wall when he heard a dry little chuckle. He snapped his eyes to the left. There, standing just behind the wall and just behind a little post that was conveniently placed, was Early. The man chuckled again. He was holding a shotgun pointed directly at Longarm. Longarm had instinctively jerked his rifle up, but now he held it very still.

Early said, "Well, I see you've come back to pay us another visit, Mr. . . . is it Long? I don't recollect exactly. It's Long or Lang or something like that."

Longarm didn't say anything. He watched the man with the shotgun. He was at a bad range to face a double-barreled shotgun. There was no way he could whip his rifle around before Early could let him have both barrels.

Early chuckled again. "Well, let's just call you Mr. Long. We're glad to welcome you back, Mr. Long, though

116

I can't quite understand what your business is here. You keep coming around telling us you are in the horse business, but Mr. Ashton didn't think so."

Longarm said, "What is this all about, Early? What do you mean, pointing that shotgun at me?"

Early laughed delightedly. "Mr. Long, you are quite the cutup, aren't you? Here you are on our property at four o'clock in the morning with a rifle in your hands, and you want to know why I am pointing a shotgun at you? Don't you reckon you can guess the answer to that one?"

Longarm said with a little edge in his voice, "If I'm disturbing anybody, I can always leave."

Early said, "Oh, I reckon you're going to be leaving, Mr. Long. I have very little doubt about that. I'm just amazed, though, that you have come to trade horses in the middle of the night. That is what you've come for, is it not? To sell us some horses?"

Longarm was watching the man steadily, his mind frantically trying to think of something he could do. "I'm here doing whatever you think I'm doing. Early."

"By the way, you wouldn't know anything about dynamite, would you?"

"I heard it will blow you up if you're not careful," Longarm said.

It made Early laugh again. "Oh, and by the way, I think it would be a lot better if you'd put that rifle down on the ground. Just let the stock rest on the ground and then just turn the barrel loose. Do you reckon you can do that, Mr. Long? This shotgun is awful heavy and it's pulling against my finger. You know how that will make a shotgun go off—your finger right there on the trigger and your finger getting heavy."

Longarm said quickly, "I'm dropping my rifle."

He let his carbine go until it dropped flat. It made a dull sound on the hardpan of the yard just short of the castle fence. Early said, "Now, that's right handsome of you, Mr. Long. Gives me a more secure feeling, if you take my meaning. I'm not really happy having a man of what I reckon your caliber might be holding a rifle that close to me, especially at this hour of the morning and with no other help around."

Longarm said, "You don't look like you'd need any help."

"Yeah, but I think you've figured out it would be better if everybody left. Was that you, Mr. Long, celebrating the Fourth of July a little early this year by setting off those dynamite charges up yonder? You know, you spooked some of the boys right bad. It was a good plan. But it didn't allow for one thing. You still had to come and you still had to get by me and you have to get to Mr. Ashton. Now, I don't know what it is that you're after, but I think we're going in the house here in a minute and talk about it. I think we're going to get you tied down in a chair somehow where we can have a real good conversation. What do you think about that, Mr. Long?"

Longarm knew one thing for certain. He was never going in that house at the point of a shotgun. Once they got him inside with a gun on him, he was as good as finished. Once they got him roped and tied down, he was definitely finished. A man could only take so much pain, and after a while, he would probably tell them nearly anything they wanted to know. He'd make up what he could, but eventually, they would just keep on because they had nothing to lose until he was whistling like the wind. He said, "Mr. Early, you are acting mighty suspicious. What do you folks have to hide here? I thought Mr. Ashton was just a rich, eccentric man who didn't like folks coming around and who liked his privacy. Do you all have something that you're doing here, that you're hiding?"

"Well, Mr. Long, I don't know that we need to discuss that much. In fact, I'll tell you what we ought to be doing right now. We ought to be getting in the house. Let's do that by you putting your hands right straight up in the air right now, Mr. Long."

Longarm put his hands slowly up to his hips. He said, "I'm not so sure that I'm comfortable with my arms up in the air. I've got a shoulder bothering me." While he was talking, he was easing his right hand around his back, enclosing it on the butt of his spare revolver.

Early said, "Mr. Long, I'm going to give you to the count of three to get your hands up in the air. I might ought to tell you that I count by twos—"

At that instant, Longarm launched himself forward in a dive, jerking out the revolver as he went. In the air, he heard the boom of the shotgun and felt the wind of the pellets going over his head. There had been only one barrel. He had his gun up now, and just before he hit the ground, he thumbed off a shot at Early, seeing the bullet taking the man in the chest. The man staggered backward. Longarm hit the ground, pulling back the hammer again. This time, he raised up slightly and fired off a second shot, hitting almost the same spot as the first one.

Early was a bigger man than Longarm had noticed the first time around, but he was also wearing a big leather coat against the cool mountain night air. He staggered back another step after the second shot, but he was still holding the shotgun. Longarm got to his knees, holding the revolver on the big man. Early was struggling. Longarm could see the effort in his face as he brought the shotgun up to his face to fire the other barrel. Just as he almost got it above the level of the wall, Longarm shot him a third time, dead center in the chest. This time, the man staggered back three steps and fell over. He fell heavily, landing with a thud. Longarm got up and walked over to the wall, his .44 cocked and held out in front of him, pointing at where the big dark figure of Early lay on the ground.

Longarm stepped over the low stone wall and walked near to where the man was lying. He kicked the shotgun a little further away. He was amazed to see that the man with three heavy slugs in his chest was still breathing. Early said, "Wha . . . Who . . . are . . ."

Longarm said, "Does it really matter, Mr. Early, who I am? You're going fast, so I reckon you don't need to know all that bad. You just made a bad mistake. You should have shot me when you had the chance."

He hadn't finished speaking when Early closed his eyes and stopped breathing. Longarm jumped back across the wall to retrieve his rifle. He took a moment to reload the empty chambers of the spare gun he had been using. He stuck it back inside his waistband at the small of his back. It was a position that seemed to work out fairly well.

Longarm took a long moment to study the big stone mansion in front of him. He knew that the shots would have been heard, but he doubted that it would make much difference. He was certain that Early had come out of the mansion when he'd been aware of Longarm's presence. Now, he was fairly certain that Ashton was alert and was preparing for his entrance. The only question was how could he best get into the castle and get at him? He wondered if Ashton had any idea what Longarm was doing and what he was after. He wondered if Ashton thought of him as someone investigating the counterfeiting. If he did, then the odds were that he would already be destroying the evidence.

But for some reason, Longarm didn't think that that was the case. Rather, Longarm figured that Ashton had him pegged as a robber, a man who had come to take some of Ashton's wealth. Longarm hadn't played the game the way a law officer would, and he didn't believe that Ashton would expect one lone United States marshal to try to infiltrate his fortress. And he certainly wouldn't have expected a federal marshal to use the methods that Longarm had used, blowing up the sides of his mountains, and especially shooting down his men. No, he had to figure that Longarm was a desperado who was after some gold or cash and didn't much care how he got it.

The one thing Longarm couldn't know for certain was whether there were any other gunmen in the house. He'd been told that there was no one else left but the women and Early. Of course, Early was no longer in the game. But Longarm doubted that Ashton could face him one against one. For that reason, he was going to be especially careful.

Longarm went back across the wall, passing Early's body, and got up next to the stone mansion. He was looking for a window or any sort of opening that would allow him to see any part of the house inside. He began skirting the place to his left. It was rectangular. He got to the corner and turned south. He came to a door, and assumed it was the back door off the kitchen. He very gently tried the knob. It felt locked. He tried no further, but kept going down the line of the building. There were any number of windows, but they were higher up than he could comfortably reach. They were all covered with some kind of curtains on the inside. The back had no other door but the kitchen door.

He turned the corner of the south side, and started down

the short side of the rectangle. He was a little surprised to see a stairwell halfway down. They were white wooden steps, and they ran up to the second story to a door. He had not expected that. For the moment, he had no intention of climbing up to the door. But it was there, and he knew it was there, and it looked like a way to get in. The only question was whether it was too obvious a way to get in.

He turned a corner again, and went down the front of the house. The first part was very much like the back, blank walls with high windows. But then he got to the porch, a big stone and concrete porch, with a good high concrete railing around it. Naturally, that led to the front door. He had been through there. The size of the door being what it was, he doubted that he could shoot his way into such a place. He did not bother to go up on the porch. Instead, he backed away from the house to get a clear view of the flat roof, to see if perhaps anyone was surveying his movements from on high. But there was nothing there, just the dark outline of the house against the dark sky.

He stood for a moment in thoughtful contemplation of the situation. Then he walked toward the south end of the mansion. He walked cautiously, looking behind him every step or two and to his open side. When he got to the end of the building, he stopped and looked carefully for a moment, searching for any sign of movement. He had decided that the stairway up to the second floor was perhaps his best method of entry. He felt pretty sure that the door at the top of the stairs would be locked. But if he had to break a door in, it was probably going to be the least conspicuous and perhaps the furtherest away from wherever Ashton and whoever was with him were located.

He slipped around the corner of the building, and went to the middle of the end wall, looking at the flight of stairs that rose up. The steps were painted white. They stood out in sharp contrast to the darker rock that made up the walls on either side. The door, he could see, did not enter straight ahead, but rather to his left. As he entered, he would be entering toward the front of the mansion. He had no idea what he would find if he were able to get the door open. He didn't know if he would be entering a bedroom, a storage room, a counterfeiting operation, or a room with more shotguns. All he knew was that he had to do something.

He started up, taking slow steps, one at a time. Surprisingly, the stair steps were wooden, but they were big heavy planks, so that they didn't creak or give. Nevertheless, he went slowly and carefully, his rifle at the ready, watching the door at the top of the landing. Every step or two, he looked behind him. If someone wanted to trap him, this was an ideal place to do it. If a figure suddenly appeared in the opening at the bottom of the stairs with a gun in his hands, he didn't much know what he could do, just try to be a little faster.

Halfway up, he could see that the door was not like the others. It was not a big, heavy, varnished affair. Rather, it too was painted white and, as near as he could make out, was made out of ordinary wood. It looked like a door you might see in a house in town. Longarm kept walking, climbing until he reached the landing. Except for the door, there was nothing else around him, just the rock of the building. The door was just there. A blank white expanse of wood. It didn't look particularly reinforced. He reached out with his right hand, holding his rifle in his left, and tentatively touched the knob. It was just a knob. With his fingers, he gave it a gentle, partial twist to the right. It went easily enough. He quickly stopped and knelt down. The door might be thin enough to fire through, and if someone saw the knob turning, they could fire through the frame of the door and kill themselves one dumb U.S. deputy marshal.

It was clear what had to be done, and he got himself ready to do it. He cocked the rifle hammer and rose from his knees so that he was on the toes of both feet. Then he made himself into as small a ball as he could. Then he reached up, turned the doorknob, and pushed the door hard.

It swung wide. The room before him was black dark. But as he looked, there suddenly came two explosions so close together that they sounded like one. There were muzzle flashes. He could hear the bullets sing over his head. Two men, two shots about four feet apart. Without aiming, he fired the rifle from his hip at where he had seen the first flash, and then levered a shell into the chamber and fired where he had seen the second muzzle flash. He dropped the rifle, drew his revolver, and fired, double-actioned, four shots, aiming low into the room. After that, he scuttled forward as fast as he could and flung himself flat.

Without further movement, he reached behind him, took the spare gun out of his waistband, and stuck the one he was using into his holster so that he had a handful of loaded gun. He had heard the distinct sound of bullet slugs hitting flesh. He had heard that sound too many times to be mistaken. It was a dull thump that only a bullet hitting something firm yet soft would give. Longarm lay quietly, holding his breath, listening as hard as he could. There was not a sound in the room. Eventually, he was going to have to find out what had happened to the men who had fired the guns at him.

Very cautiously, he got to one knee, the revolver pointed in the general direction where he had seen the guns fired. He reached into his shirt pocket and got out one of the big matches he had been using to light the dynamite. He felt the floor. It was hardwood. Longarm pulled back the hammer on his revolver. When he struck the match, he wouldn't have much time to think about what to do.

In the sudden blaze of light that the match made, he saw one man lying flat on his face, a gun held loosely in his hand. He wasn't moving or breathing. There was a door on the other side of the room that was half open. There was no one else there. Longarm did not believe that the man on the floor had fired one shot and then jumped four feet to the other side and fired another. He walked across the little room, looking. Sure enough, leading through the door he could see a pattern of bloodstains that someone had left from a wound that was leaking, most likely, from a .44 cartridge.

Longarm struck another match and looked down at the dead man. He was just ordinary-looking. He could have been one of those that had met him and had been sent to kill him. He looked like all the rest of those young, hard ranch hands that Ashton had hired.

The only problem was that he wasn't supposed to be there. According to the men he'd talked to, there was nobody left but Early, but there was one and there was one that had gotten away. The question was, how many more of them were between him and Ashton and the counterfeiting?

Longarm pushed the half-open door open fully. Again, there was the dark. He crouched swiftly, but no gunshots rang out. Instead, he noticed a pencil-thin line of light running along the floor a few feet to his right. From other speckles of light running up toward the ceiling, he could tell it was a door into a lighted room. It gave him pause. He had no idea what opening that door was going to uncover. For a moment he stood in the anteroom that lay between the two rooms. Finally, he shrugged. With his revolver at the ready and the rifle in his hand, cocked and loaded, he reached out and felt around gingerly until he located the knob. It too turned easily to his touch. He shoved at the door with a quick hard motion, leaning hard up against the wall as he did so as to be as much out of the line of fire as possible. Nothing happened.

He carefully put his eye around the doorjamb. Just across the room, some fourteen feet by fourteen feet, he saw a man lying on his back, propped up against the wall next to yet another door. The man had a grimace on his face and both of his hands were clutching his thigh. Longarm could see the trail of blood on the floor that led out of the room he had just left and to under the man's leg where he lay. He had a gun, but it was a few feet away on the floor. Longarm moved in swiftly, holding his rifle at the ready. The man just glanced up at him and grimaced.

Longarm leaned down and flipped the man's revolver away. Then he looked at another one of the hard-faced young gunmen who had hired out to Ashton. The gunman looked steadily back at him. He said, his voice choking, "I'm bleeding to death. You've got to get me some help."

Longarm stood looking down at him. He nodded slowly. "Yeah, I guarantee you're bleeding to death and you ain't far to go. You should have put a tourniquet on that."

The young man's face twisted. "I don't know how," he said.

"Tell you what. I'll put one on you if you'll tell me what's ahead and where Ashton is and what I've got to go through to get to him. Is that a deal?"

The man nodded quickly. "Hell, yes. What choice do I have?"

Longarm said, "You have the choice between lying and telling the truth. If you lie, I'll find out about it and I'll come back and undo any good I've done. Do you understand that?"

The man said, "I don't owe that sonofabitch nothing. He paid us a little extra to stay on and try to stop you. He didn't think you were very smart."

Longarm half smiled. "I don't reckon you boys who've been working for him ought to be talking about who's smart and who's not."

"Damn it! Are you going to help me or not?" The man raised a weak voice. "I'm bleeding!"

Longarm reached into his pocket and took out his big clasp knife. He opened the blade, and the man stared at him, frightened.

Longarm said, "Don't get nervous. I ain't fixing to stick you. I've got to find something to make a tourniquet out of, and I was thinking about your sleeve. Wait a minute, what size belt are you wearing on your britches?" He reached down, lifted the man's gun belt up, and looked at the belt that was run through the loops of his jeans. It was a narrow belt about the right size. He unbuckled it and pulled it, with some effort, out from under the man. After that, he quickly ran it under the man's leg and worked it up until it was up to the very top of his thigh. Longarm buckled it back again, but there was a great deal of slack in it. He needed something to twist it with. The room had several packing crates in it with wooden slats. With the butt of his rifle, he busted one of the slats, got it loose, and worked it off, and then with his knife, peeled it down until it was not quite the size of a twelve-inch ruler. He ran that through the looped belt and twisted it until it began to put a pressure on the man's groin. He knew that was where the big blood vessel was, and he knew that was where you had to shut the blood off.

The man's face was going chalky white. His eyes were afraid. "Is it doing any good?" He had taken his hands away so Longarm could work, and the blood had almost been gurgling out when Longarm first started putting the tourniquet on. Now that he had it tight, the blood ceased to flow. Longarm guided the man's hand to the piece of wood. He said, "You've got to keep this tight. This is what is shutting off the blood and keeping it inside you so that it can't run out that hole in your leg. It's got to coagulate. Now, you've got a rough time ahead of you. Tell me the truth so I can get my business cleared up, and then I can get back here and bandage you better. What you need is that doctor in town, but you couldn't get there by yourself."

The man's face was still pale. He said, "Has it stopped bleeding?"

"Yes, but you've lost a lot of blood. I don't understand what you two were doing in that room in there."

The man said through clenched teeth, "We were just supposed to watch that door in there and shoot anybody who came through it. That's all we were told. Mr. Early gave us an extra hundred dollars apiece for staying on for a couple more days. If we plugged you—I reckon it was you—we were going to get an extra five hundred, so naturally we jumped at the chance."

"All right. What other surprises do I have? First of all, where is Ashton?"

"As far as I know, he's in his big office," the man said. "Do you know where that is?"

"Yeah, it's downstairs on the other end of the house."

"That's right."

128

"Who else is here?"

"Well, there is his woman and her servant. She may be the woman's aunt for all I know. And then there is two men downstairs."

"Is that all?"

The man nodded slowly. "Yeah, that's all. All the other women left."

Longarm said, "They told me there was five men trying to get out. That only accounts for four."

"Early shot the other one. Slim somebody. He wouldn't go along with it. Said he'd get out somehow. Early shot him with that shotgun of his, I reckon as some encouragement to us so we'd give him a helping hand."

"What kind of hands are those boys downstairs?"

"Good ones."

Longarm said, "Where are they?"

"I think both of them are watching the back door. One of them may be watching the front door. Early was real certain that the attack would come from the staircase you came up."

Longarm stood up, wiping his hands, where he had gotten some blood on them, on his jeans. "Well, here's what you need to do. I don't know if you can tell when fifteen minutes is up, but you need to loosen that tourniquet for about two or three minutes. If you don't, you'll get gangrene in your leg. Then you tighten it up for another fifteen minutes. Understand that?"

"Hell, are you going to be gone that long?"

Longarm shrugged. "It depends on how long it takes me to do my business. Do you know where they keep the counterfeiting machinery?"

The man gave him a blank look. "The what?"

"Where they make those counterfeit twenty-dollar bills."

The wounded man shook his head back and forth slowly. He said, "Mister, I don't know what you're talking about. Counterfeit twenty-dollar bills? I've never heard of such a thing."

Longarm believed him. It was very possible for only a few select individuals to carry on a counterfeiting operation. There was no need for even the guards to know what they were guarding. He started toward the door, carrying his rifle loosely in his left hand. He said, "Where does this door go?"

The man on the floor said, his voice getting weaker, "It shoots over to the main hall. Take it over to the big staircase. That will take you right into Mr. Ashton's office. I don't know where the other two men are, so don't hold me accountable. When you go through that door, I reckon you better be looking both ways."

Longarm stepped to the door with his rifle in his right hand. He reached out with his left and turned the knob. The door opened inward, and he pulled it to him, letting it go by him. The hall was alight with lanterns hanging from the ceiling. He took a quick look around the door frame. It was a small hall, and empty. He walked a few steps to the one door that led off it. Again, he followed the same procedure. As he held the rifle at his ready, he turned the knob and pulled it to him. Again, there was nothing but empty space.

This time, the door had opened onto the main upstairs hallway. It was a good eight feet wide and long. At the other end, he could see the curved banister of the stairs where he had seen the beautiful Spanish-looking young woman a few days before. The hall was lit with several chandeliers. He guessed it to be about twenty-five feet long.

He moved slowly. There were two doors that opened off to each side.

He came to the first door on his left, and eased his rifle to his right hand and then pushed open the door with his left. It was dark. In the dimness, he could see the outline of a canopy bed and other furniture. He could see no movement. He pulled the door to, and then opened the one across from it. The room was practically empty, with only a few chairs and a table. He didn't know its purpose. Then he came to the second door on his left. He opened it. Much like the first one, this was also a bedroom. Both of the rooms were big, just as one would expect for such a large house. After he looked the big room over, he pulled the door to as he had the other ones. If someone were to slip up behind him, if he had overlooked them, he wanted at least some sound when they emerged.

He turned, and was about to go to the next door on his right when it suddenly opened. He jerked the rifle up into a firing position, his finger on the trigger. He froze, staring in amazement.

It was the Spanish girl. She just stood there, wearing a very thin housedress. It could just as easily been a bed gown, except that it buttoned up the front. She stood there, staring at him. Staring hard. For a second, Longarm didn't know what to say. Then he stammered out, "Excuse me. I'm mighty sorry if I've disturbed you. I . . . uh . . . I was looking for . . . uh . . . Mr. Ashton."

She didn't bother to answer him. Instead, she stepped out of the room and came directly toward him. As she moved, she put her hands up and began unbuttoning the flimsy dress. It was so thin, he could see the nipples of her breast through the material and see the dark patch of pubic hair at her crotch. He could feel his groin swell, and feel that copper taste come into his mouth. Her eyes were riveted on his, holding him tightly with her look. He sat the rifle down by his boot, not knowing what to do.

Now, she was pressing her body up against him. She reached up and pulled his head down and kissed him full on the mouth. He could feel the softness of her lips and the wetness of her tongue. He could feel himself growing too small in that space in his jeans. But he had no time for this. He could feel her arms going around his neck. He tried to pull away. This was absurd. He was able to pull his mouth away in order to say, "Miss, miss. What are you doing?"

But she was putting her hands on his member, rubbing him with her nimble fingers. It was impossible for him not to come to full erection. He could feel her fingers fumbling at his buttons. She was pulling him down, down, down toward the floor just with the weight of her arms around his neck. He didn't know what to do. The next thing he knew, his member was free and she was holding it in her hands. She had pulled him down to his knees and she was on hers, and then she somehow rolled onto her back, opening her legs and pulling him onto her.

His head was afire. His senses reeled. He couldn't think. He heard the thud as he dropped his rifle. Then all he knew was that she was guiding him into her. He could see the flash of white skin and the pink depths that awaited him. He tried to regain control of the situation. He was in the middle of the hall in the enemy's house with this girl. It was no time to be doing what he was doing. Ever since he had stood at the door at the top of the stairs, the hair at the back of his neck had been up. Now, it was rising even more. Almost as if by instinct, he glanced up. There was a man at the head of the stairway. He had a rifle in his hand.

Without pause, Longarm jerked the revolver out of his

holster and flung himself flat on top of the girl. He fired just as the man brought the rifle to his shoulder. Longarm saw the slug catch the man in the middle of his belly. It had not been the shot he had wanted, but it did have the effect of ruining the man's aim. The rifle fired, but the bullet went whining overhead helplessly. The hard-faced young man had taken a step backward. He tried to lever another shell into the chamber. Longarm took careful aim this time, and fired. The bullet caught the man in the chest and he staggered back, his spine against the railing of the stairs. He stood there, his fingers dropping the rifle on the hard wooden floor. It clattered noisily. He turned to try and walk down the stairs. Longarm shot him again. This time, he could see the bullet hit the man in the shoulder. It spun the man around and he went falling, tumbling down the winding staircase.

Longarm stood up. His erection was gone. He looked down at the woman lying on the floor. Her dress was still up around her hips and for an instant, he admired the view. She had unbuttoned her dress enough so that her breasts were showing. They were big and taut and tight. They were just the way he liked them, with big brown nipples.

He said formally, buttoning his pants, ''Ma'am, I'm right sorry, but I'm busy right now. Maybe we can finish this business a little bit later.''

Then he stepped past her, over her leg, and went down the hall, his revolver at the ready. He had picked up the rifle, but he was carrying it loosely in his left hand. It was getting too close for rifle work. He figured the rest of the way, he'd be using a pistol, but he didn't want to leave the rifle with the girl. She apparently was capable in more than one way. She had nearly done him in with her body. He didn't want her to do him in with his own rifle.

He found the gunman dead halfway down the stairs. Longarm took a moment to pick up the man's rifle and jack all the shells out of it before slinging it back down near the man's body. He took the man's pistol as well, and emptied the cartridges out. Then he took time to reload his own revolver. As far as he knew, there was one man left. He didn't know who he was or where he was, but Longarm hoped he wouldn't be hiding behind the skirts of some really good-looking woman.

Longarm finished the descent of the staircase, and stood in the big hall. He knew to his immediate left was the big library and then Ashton's office. But he didn't know what was ahead and to the right. He thought there was a back door, and perhaps that was where the other gunman was waiting. He was still shaken by the near calamity of the gunman and the woman. More than anything else, it struck him as a hell of a way to get killed, in a hell of a position and a hell of an activity. If the story ever got out about him like that, he might as well be dead because he'd never be able to live it down. He had enough of a reputation with the ladies as it was, and there was no need for a story to get out that he had died in the saddle, so to speak.

He decided he would check to the right first. He pushed under the stairs and to some big double doors. He opened one of them slowly. It was dark inside, and he ducked down and half crawled into the room to get his bearings. It would be a good place for an ambush. When his eyes adjusted, he could see a long table and a number of chairs. It was a dining room. He kept looking around. He could see a door that opened toward a back wall. That should be the kitchen, but he couldn't be certain.

He rose to his feet and walked around the dining room table to the left. When he reached the swinging door that led to the kitchen, he hunkered down again and slowly pushed it open. It was dark inside, but warmer, and had the smell of a place where food was prepared. He got just inside the door, sweeping the room with his pistol and his rifle. There was not a sign of anyone there.

He continued on around the dining room table until he came to the door on the opposite side of the room. It too was a big double door. He pulled one side open toward him, ducking as he did. Just as he guessed, it led into the front parlor. There was a little light coming through the front windows, and he could see better. It was a big formal affair with a lot of overstuffed furniture. It didn't look like it got much use. Now, Longarm was ready to check out the part of the house that he thought might prove more interesting.

He walked back down the dining room table, and exited quickly out the door, half expecting to be met by someone who had observed his entrance into the room. There was no one there. He was in a small hall-like area, with a door immediately to his right that either went to a room or went outside. He thought there was a back door, and he thought there was a man watching it.

Longarm could feel the hair prickling on the back of his neck again. He looked at the door. It was just an ordinary door, but he had a feeling that it was a very dangerous door. He thought there would be some close work inside, so he leaned his rifle against the wall, reached around to his rear belt, and pulled out his spare revolver. He checked it again to make sure it was loaded, and then drew his other revolver out of the holster. He wanted to have all the firepower he could. He reached out and gently turned the doorknob as he had before. He pushed the door, ducking down again as he did.

Nothing happened. He was just in a small dark room, lit partially by the light behind him. The only thing he could tell was that it was some sort of storage area for the kitchen, since there were cases of canned foods, sacks of flour, sacks of dried beans and peas and other bulk food. Just ahead was another door, this one with a glass in the top. He eased over to it, bending down, and tried to see through the window glass. He couldn't tell where it went. It could have been the door to the outside. He couldn't imagine why you would put a window glass in the top half of an interior door, but then he couldn't be sure. The hair was still standing up on the back of his neck. He gripped his revolvers more closely and squatted down just to the left of the door. With his right hand, he carefully turned the knob and then swiftly drew the door back.

Chapter 8

The black night was suddenly lit by the twin muzzle blast of a double-barrel shotgun. Longarm could feel the full charge of pellets go whistling right over his head. Instinctively, he fired with his left hand. His right hand, holding the other revolver, was still shoving the door aside. He felt as if something had tugged at his arm as the charge had gone overhead.

Now, he fired again at where the barrel blast had been. He fired with his left revolver and then with his right hand, shooting two, three, four, five times. He heard a moan, then a sigh, and then the soft sound of something collapsing. He was outside. The steps led down to the ground. He went slowly, aware that he only had three or four cartridges in his guns. He was amazed that he'd had to fire so many times to hit the man. But then, in a few steps, he discovered the reason why.

There was a large wooden box sitting just a few feet from the back door. It was about four feet high and about four feet wide. It apparently contained some kind of machinery, since it had shipping stickers all over it. Behind it lay another one of the hard-faced narrow-eyed gunslingers that

Ashton seemed to have cut out with a cookie cutter. Longarm walked around the box that the man had been hiding behind and looked down at him. It was coming now toward dawn, and Longarm could make him out quite distinctly. He stirred him with the toe of his boot, but the man was dead. He turned and went back up the steps through the back door of the house, through the dark room, and back out into the wide hall underneath the stairs. To his right was a library, and beyond that was supposedly Ashton. If the man who was bleeding to death was telling him the truth, he had killed the last of the four gunmen.

He wondered what surprises Ashton was going to have in store for him.

Longarm walked over to the big double doors that led into the library, and twisted the knob of one handle. He pushed the door back. It was big and heavy, but it rode smoothly on its hinges. As it opened, he stepped further away from the entrance just in case there was somebody there, waiting to fire. He had one gun in his holster now and the other in his hand. He took time to reload. It almost emptied his pockets. Now, with just one revolver in his right hand, he started forward. He could see the door beyond the big library that led into Ashton's office. It was outlined by the light from within.

Longarm had taken several steps into the library when he felt someone behind him. He whirled, and suddenly felt soft arms going around his neck and moist, soft lips pressing against his. It was the girl again. He kept both hands up in the air trying to pull away from her, but she was holding him, her arms encircling his neck, her mouth glued to his. He stumbled on the rug, his spurs dragging in the thick carpet. To catch himself, he went down to his knees. She was with him. He glanced toward the open door of the library, but there was no one there. He turned his head with some difficulty, since the girl was holding him so tight, and looked toward Ashton's office. He had not opened the door.

Longarm shoved the revolver back in his waistband, and then got ahold of the girl's wrists and unwrapped them around his neck. He said in a very fierce whisper to her, "Please, not now. I'm as busy as hell."

She was panting and trying to kiss him in the ear. She said, "Yes, yes, I must have. Yes."

He said, "No, will you please wait. Go back upstairs and wait. I haven't got time for you right now." He got to his feet and holding her by her wrists, pulled and dragged her to the door of the library and shoved her out into the hall. Then he shut the library door. There was a lock on it. He turned it.

He shook himself as if to shake the feel and the smell of the girl off his body. Then he strolled purposefully across the library floor, walking soundlessly on the heavy carpet. He pulled out his waistband revolver as he neared the door. It was clearly lit inside the room. The outline of light traced the big heavy door. Longarm stood there, wondering exactly how he was going to get inside. As far as he could remember, it was a completely closed office, even without a window. He stood there, thinking. Finally, with the muzzle of his revolver, he knocked on the door.

There was no answer except silence.

He knocked again, harder this time.

A moment passed, and then a low voice, perhaps hushed by the thickness of the wall and the door, said, "Who is it?"

Longarm recognized Ashton's voice. He said, "You know damned good and well who it is. It's Custis Long. Now, let me in there."

"I don't have time right now, Mr. Long. Could you come back tomorrow?"

Longarm gazed in amazement at the door as if he could see the face of the man who would have made such a statement.

He said, "Are you crazy? Open this damned door."

There was no sound from within. Longarm turned the knob. It turned about an inch, and then stopped. It was locked.

Longarm beat on the door again. He said, "Ashton, open this damned door. You can't get out of there. Do you want me to start shooting through this door?"

Ashton answered back. "The door's too thick."

Longarm stood there, puzzling over what to do. He wasn't sure he could shoot the lock loose, but it was the only choice he had. He stepped back, narrowed his eyes in case there was any flying metal, and fired at the base of the doorknob. He fired once, then twice. On the third shot, he saw the door move inward. With a hard kick, he sent it crashing around. He was suddenly framed in an open door with his drawn pistol aimed at a man behind his desk. It was Ashton.

Longarm could see that both of his hands were empty. He looked frightened. He didn't look very big.

Ashton said, "You can't come in here. It's against the law."

Longarm reached in his pocket and took out his badge. He said, "Ashton, I am the law. The name is Custis Long, but that's United States Deputy Marshal Custis Long. And you're a counterfeiter and that's against the law and we're going to talk about it. Now, you are under arrest. Stand up."

He walked into the room as Ashton came to his feet.

Longarm quickly looked to the left to make sure there was no one else in the office. It was empty. Finally, somehow, he had managed to get alone with the man that he set out to get alone. He had run his counterfeiter to the ground, he hoped.

Longarm said, "Get your hands up in the air."

Ashton was wearing a brocaded silver-colored vest and a white shirt, his graying hair was nattily combed, and he was clean-shaven. He hardly looked like a man who was getting ready for a fight. But then Ashton had never planned to do any of the fighting. His finely drawn features and delicate hands were not meant for the rough-and-tumble work. They were meant for the engraving of counterfeit plates or the cutting of paper that closely resembled that used by the United States Government.

Longarm sat down in a chair in front of the desk while Ashton slowly raised his hands.

Ashton said, "I've got a sore shoulder. This is going to cause me extreme discomfort. I don't want to hold my hands up like this."

Longarm said, "I'm not going to let you sit down at the desk with all those drawers in there where you probably have a dozen hideout guns." To his left was a small wooden table with two chairs. He gestured with his gun. "Come around here and sit in that yonder chair, the one against the wall. I'll take the one facing you." He walked over to where he had indicated, and waited as Ashton came around and sat down carefully in the chair opposite his.

Longarm put his revolver butt on the top of the round table with the barrel pointing directly at Ashton. With his thumb, he cocked the revolver.

Ashton shuddered. He said, "Oh, please don't do that. It makes me very nervous."

"Well, you're going to be a whole lot more nervous unless you tell me right quick where all the paraphernalia is that you use to counterfeit twenty-dollar bills."

Ashton's face didn't change in the slightest. He said, "I don't know what you're talking about. I don't know anything about counterfeiting."

Longarm sighed. "Of course, I knew you were going to say that. And of course, I don't believe you. So, I guess we're going to have to do this the hard way. I reckon you'll have it that way, won't you, Mr. Ashton?"

"I tell you, I don't know anything about counterfeiting."

Longarm laughed. "Then would you mind telling me how you've been paying forty gunhands and you're not running a single cow on this beautiful piece of grassland? Would you mind telling me what you are doing sitting up here in this castle and who bought it and what with? Would you mind telling me what you do at this out-of-the-way place?"

Ashton swallowed hard. "I . . . I inherited money. It was my money."

Longarm gave the man a mild look. "Did you need all these gunhands to protect it? Couldn't you have put it in the bank or buried it out in the backyard or something? What were all the gunhands for, Mr. Ashton?"

"I . . . I . . . it wasn't my idea to hire them. Mr. Early thought they would be decorative."

"Decorative?"

"Yes, uh, to . . . make the place look like a real working ranch. Yes, that's it."

Longarm said, "Ashton, you are lying. I know you're lying. We both know you're lying. Why don't you save us both some trouble and give up that paraphernalia you've got that you make the bills with?"

"That would be illegal. I'm not an illegal man. I inherited my money."

Longarm sighed. He said, "I hate to tell you this, but I'm afraid we're going to have to get to the point where we do a little hurting. You see, I didn't want this assignment in the first place. I didn't want to have to come down here. I knew it was going to be a lot of trouble. I knew it was going to be hard to get to you, and I knew I was going to have to kill a lot of people to get to you. Sure enough, all of that came true. Finally, I got to the point where it is just me and you, and believe me, Mr. Ashton, I'm going to have the truth out of you before I'm done. Do you understand that? Do you understand that I've got no choice except to make you tell me where that stuff is?"

Ashton looked frightened. He said, "What did you do with Mr. Early?"

"I killed him along with the four men you had in the house that were supposed to stop me. There is nobody but you and me, and I've got the gun and I'm bigger and I'm stronger and I'm meaner. So, you are going to tell me. It may take a while. You might lose some teeth. You might lose an ear. You might lose a finger. Lord, I don't know what you might lose. You might lose your balls. Before it's over with, you're going to hurt bad enough that you're going to want to tell me. Like I said, this ain't supposed to be my job. I don't like it, so I'm going to get it over with just as fast as I can."

Ashton looked frightened, but he still said, "I'm not a counterfeiter and I don't know what you're talking about. I have lived here quietly for a number of years. I am a stockman. I was going to stock this place with cattle. I had nothing to do with counterfeiting money."

Longarm was still pointing his revolver directly at the

143

man's chest. Ashton had both of his hands lying on top of the small, round, varnished table. Longarm did not know if Ashton had a weapon concealed about his person, but he doubted it, although it didn't make much difference anyway, as long as Ashton kept his hands where they were. He took a second to remind the man of that. He said, "I want your hands where I can see them, Mr. Ashton. In fact, I like them just the way they are, palms downward, flat on that table. Unless you know how to shoot a gun with your boot, I think we'll get along all right."

Ashton said with fear in his eyes, "Do you have to point that revolver at me? Can't you point it in some other direction?"

"I want you to get used to it, Mr. Ashton. You see the hammer's back. My finger is inside the trigger guard on the trigger. It wouldn't take much more than a sneeze and this thing would go off and blow your chest completely through the back of your chair."

Ashton let out a small scream. He said, "That's exactly what I mean. What if you coughed or something? For God's sake, son, point that gun in some other direction."

Longarm said, smiling, "It ain't bothering me. But what is bothering me is when are you going to tell me where it was that you did your counterfeiting? Where are the plates and the paper and the presses that you run those twenty-dollar bills off on? You're going to have to show me sooner or later. And right now would be the best time. It's daylight now. You can't tell it in this room, but I would imagine that the sun's up by now. There might be some people curious as to what's going on out here. If they should happen to come out here, I'd hate to think what might happen to you. You see, I'm a law officer, so I'm within my rights."

"You can't torture me then. If you're an officer of the law, you have no right to torture me."

Longarm yawned. "It's been a long night, Ashton. I'm getting damned tired. Now, I ain't going to torture you, but I am going to persuade the hell out of you. If you think about it for a minute, that's all I'm going to do is persuade you. Now, where is all that paraphernalia and your print shop for that counterfeiting?"

Ashton said, "I don't know of anything."

Longarm had been looking at Ashton's right hand. The little finger looked to be just about the right diameter. He thought it would frighten the man considerably if he was afraid of the open mouth of the revolver staring at him. He wondered what he would look like with a finger sticking up the revolver.

He moved his revolver forward, and then suddenly reached out and clamped a hard hand over Ashton's smaller and more delicate one. The man tried to jerk backward, but Longarm held him fast. With a rigid grip on his hand, he managed to pull the little finger free from the rest of the hand. He pulled Ashton's hand forward with his left hand while at the same time, he pushed his revolver closer and closer until the little finger went into the muzzle of the revolver almost up to the middle joint.

Ashton screamed in short, staccato bursts and tried to jump around. Longarm said, "Damn you, you'd better be still. I've got my finger inside this trigger guard, and if you get to jumping around much more, this thing is going to get loose and blow your finger off."

"You can't do this," Ashton said in an agonizing voice. "You'll ruin my finger! My God, what can I do if you shoot my finger off?"

"You agree to tell me where that stuff is and I'll agree to let you get your finger out of there."

It was at the instant that Ashton looked up sharply. Longarm couldn't turn his head, but he heard a light rapping at the door. At that instant, Ashton screamed, "Help! Help!" and jerked his hand back. The problem was that the muzzle was caught on the second knuckle and as Ashton jerked his hand back, it pulled at the pistol. It wasn't much, but it was enough for the hair-trigger touch of Longarm's revolver. The gun roared with a little of Ashton's finger still in the muzzle. The blast came right under Longarm's hand and wrist. He could feel the heat.

But Ashton felt the bullet take off part of his finger. He screamed and yelled and jumped straight up in the air, and went dashing around the table toward the back of the office, holding his wounded hand aloft. He was screaming, "Help! Help! I'm killed! I'm dying!"

Longarm got up and chased him for a moment before he could corner him. The hand didn't look too bad, though the tip of the finger had been shot away. There wasn't much blood. There were no big arteries or veins in the little finger. But he couldn't do anything for Ashton, or to him, as long as he was hysterical. With resignation, Longarm sighed and hit the man a hard jolt on the jaw. Ashton dropped out cold. Longarm caught him just before he hit the floor. He dragged him over to a settee and laid him out full length. He noticed a silk scarf in the man's sleeve, and he pulled it out and bound up the little finger as best as he could. He could tell that it wasn't ever going to be quite the same, even though no more than a half inch had been blown away, but he did imagine it was painful. He reckoned that anytime you stuck your finger in the muzzle of a gun and it went off, it would be somewhat painful.

He knew that Ashton would be waking soon and that he was going to be screaming his head off in agony. He went quickly to Ashton's desk, and looked through the drawers until he found two bottles of brandy and a couple of glasses. He set them on the small table. Then he fetched Ashton the way you would a child, and placed him in the chair, letting his head fall forward on the table. He carefully put Ashton's hand out where it would be in as comfortable a position as possible. On a thought, he went to the settee and brought a cushion over to put Ashton's hand on. Then Longarm sat back down on the chair across from the counterfeiter. Ashton wouldn't be out very long, and when he came to, he would be hurting. In fact, he would probably be hurting so bad that the threat of more pain wouldn't scare him that much.

Longarm had to have some lever, some come-a-long to make him reveal the hiding place of his counterfeiting operation. But he was afraid he was going to have to bide his time. That was exactly what he didn't want to do. He was sick of this place, sick of this ranch, sick of this house, and most of all, sick of this job that wasn't his to do. It wasn't in his line. He chased bank robbers, he chased rustlers, he chased murderers, he chased men who were used to a fight. This little fool across the table from him was just a kid on a sugar tit.

Longarm glared at Vernon Ashton as he thought. The whiskey wasn't going to help the pain very much. It would help a little, but not much. But besides that, it was just brandy. It didn't pack the wallop of that good Maryland whiskey he had back at the hotel.

Just as he was muttering about what he was going to do, he became aware of the faint knocking at the door again.

He whirled around, uncertain of what he'd heard. The knocking came again.

It was hard for him to believe. The only thing he could think of was that it was that damned girl again. Would she never stop and leave him alone again until this whole business was over? If she would do that, he'd be more than happy to give her what she wanted.

The continued knocking irritated him. He jerked out his pistol and yelled, "Come in, damn it! Come in."

Chapter 9

The door was just slightly ajar. Someone gave it a faint push, and it swung wide open. But instead of the girl or anyone else that Longarm was going to use his pistol on, there stood the short, slightly fat Chinese man in his white coat and little black hat, with a pigtail coming out from beneath that. He had his hands folded over his round belly, and he bowed several times before he spoke.

The Chinese man said, "So sorry. Think maybe you need some one little thing."

Longarm just stared at him. "What?"

"Think you catch some good eats. Fix you some good meal? Okay? For you and boss?"

It should have been obvious to the man, Longarm thought, that his boss was laying face-down on the small rosewood table with his right hand all bandaged up in his own silk scarf. But the man didn't seem to get it. Longarm said, "You want to fix us some food?"

The Chinese man nodded his head. "Yes, me fix food. Catch good meal."

Longarm scratched his head. He wasn't at all hungry, but

a thought had occured to him. "You savvy laudanum? White stuff in little bottle?"

The little man nodded his head vigorously. "Ah . . . soo . . . Yes, me catch laudrum for bad hurt. Yes, me catch."

Longarm said, glancing around at Vernon Ashton, "Then chop, chop. Bring it back here. Chop, chop."

The little man went shuffling off, his slippers making very little sound on the carpeted floor of the library. Longarm was doubtful that he really understood about the laudanum, but if he could produce some, it would go a long way toward helping him with Vernon Ashton.

He looked over at his suspect. Ashton was beginning to groan and move his head slightly. In another moment or two, the man would be fully conscious and yelling his head off about what remained of his little finger. It was going to be very difficult to get him to talk while he was hurting so bad. In preparation for his awakening, Longarm poured out a big drink of brandy in both glasses, one for himself and one for Ashton when he was awake enough to take it. But Longarm saw no reason to wait himself. It had already been a long enough night that he figured he had earned a drink or two. He put the glass to his lips and took it down in one long shot. It made a very satisfying glow as it ran down his gullet and spread around in his stomach. He poured his glass full again, watching Vernon Ashton, waiting for him to come awake. He reached into his pocket, pulled out a cigarillo, and lit it with a match. It tasted very satisfying. Of course, what would have tasted even more satisfying was a steak and some fried eggs. He realized that maybe he was getting pretty hungry, but there would be no time until he got his hands on what he wanted.

To his surprise, the Chinese man was back before he expected. Vernon Ashton was moving around when Longarm noticed the houseboy come shuffling across the library, a small glass bottle in his hand. Longarm could even see that it was full of white liquid. In another moment, the little man came through the door.

Longarm said, "Let's see what you have there." He put out his hand.

"Me catch laudrum," the little man said. "Like you say. Laudrum for big hurt."

Longarm took the bottle and turned it. Indeed it was labeled as laundanum, and was from a pharmacy. "Well, I believe you. Damn right, this is the real stuff." He took the glass stopper out and smelled it. It smelled like what he remembered laudanum smelled like. "Very good. You did very good. What is your name?"

"My name is Lei Chang. I make meals, serve the boss. You want me to fix some things to eat?"

Longarm said, "No, you better wait outside. I still need to talk to Mr. Ashton. Just close the door after you when you leave."

Longarm waited a moment until Lei Chang was out of the room and had pulled the door somewhat closed. He turned and poured a good dollop of the laudanum into the glass of brandy he had poured for Ashton. He thought if he could get it down the man, it would knock out the worst part of the pain.

Ashton sat up slowly and opened his eyes. He blinked for a second, looking around as if he wasn't quite certain where or who he was. There was an angry red blotch on his left jaw where Longarm had punched him to knock him out. With his left hand, he reached up and worked the jaw back and forth for a second, a wondering look in his eye. Then Vernon Ashton glanced down at his hand and saw the kerchief around his little finger. He blinked. He said, slurring his words, "Is that blood?"

Longarm put the drink right in front of the man, and said, "You're fixing to start hurting pretty bad here in a moment. You'd better drink this."

For answer, Vernon Ashton suddenly let out a howl. He screamed, "My God, you've shot my finger off! You sonofabitch! My God, you've killed me! Oh, it hurts!"

Longarm pushed the drink closer to the man's left hand. He said, "Drink this quick."

Vernon Ashton was rolling around in his own pain. He said, "Oh, hell, this hurts. You sonofabitch, you stuck my finger in your gun and shot it off."

Little by little, Longarm was able to convince the man that if he would drink the mixture of brandy and laudanum down, he would feel better. Finally, with a trembling hand, Ashton got the glass up and drank off about a third of it.

Longarm urged him on. He half rose from his seat and put out his hand to support Ashton's wrist as he said, "Drink it all. It'll save you a lot of pain."

With a trembling hand that spilled some of the mixture, Ashton got the glass to his lips again and finished it off. Immediately, Longarm poured the glass half full of brandy and put in a little more laudanum. He didn't know how much it was safe to take, but he was going to get this man out of his pain to where he could concentrate on where the counterfeiting paraphernalia was located if it killed him. He didn't want him distracted by a little thing like a shot-off finger.

Ashton's face was still full of pain, but it was clear that the mixture of alcohol and the potent drug was starting to take effect. He had ceased to moan and wail, and now he took the second glass down with a swift move. This time, Longarm refilled it with only brandy.

Vernon Ashton stared at Longarm. He said, "Didn't you show me a badge? Didn't you say you were a United States deputy marshal? A lawman?"

Longarm nodded slowly.

"Then what gives you the right to torture me like you just did? You're more outlaw than you are law."

Longarm said, "Mr. Ashton, you made me just more than a little mad when you dismissed me out of here the other day and were going to have me shot just because I didn't measure up to your idea of what a horse trader was supposed to know. It happens that I am a horse trader, but I've never bred the kind of stock you were talking about, so if I'd really been some horse trader coming by here and not a man able to take care of himself, you'd have had your boys drag me up there in those rocks and leave me where the crows could pick the meat off my bones. Now, ain't that a fact?"

Ashton grimaced. Longarm couldn't tell if it was from the pain or from being faced with his own actions. The man said, "I had nothing to do with that. Early was the man who gave that order."

Longarm looked at him dryly. "And who did Mr. Early work for?"

"That had nothing to do with it."

"Oh, I reckon we both know it had everything to do with it. You gave the order to Early. Or was it just a standing order? If you didn't like somebody, take the sonofabitch out and shoot him, is that it? Early is just the one that did the job so you didn't get your delicate little fingers soiled."

"You wait until I tell them about you shooting off one of my fingers. You are going to be in big trouble."

153

Longarm put his revolver back on the table. "Maybe all the shooting ain't done yet, Mr. Ashton. You've lost one finger. Do you want to try for two?"

Vernon Ashton cringed backward in his chair. "You wouldn't dare! You are a horrible beast! But even you wouldn't be that cruel. You couldn't do that again."

Longarm smiled at him. "You just try me, Ashton. Now, you are going to show me where you've got this counterfeiting operation if I've got to take your fingers off one at a time."

"You are acting illegally. You know it's illegal for you to even be here. You have no right here. You came on this property masquerading as something you're not. You never declared you were a lawman."

Longarm took a drag on his cigarillo, which was still burning. He said, "Ashton, in your particular case, I don't plan on following none of the rules. I've got a personal feeling toward you that's even beyond my duties as a law officer. Now, you have defrauded an awful lot of innocent folks that can't afford to lose twenty dollars. The word I got from the boys in the Treasury Department was that a whole lot of folks had to turn in those phony twenty-dollar bills and they didn't get anything in return. And then there's that busines about you were going to kill me. I guess you can see that I'm just not real pleased with you. You might also see where it doesn't make me any difference how I have to operate to get your cooperation. Do you take my meaning? Now, how is it going to be? Do you want to get another finger in the wrong place, or do you want to show me where that operation is that you make that phony money?"

Ashton was full enough of the laudanum and brandy that he was getting whiskey-brave. He drew himself up and

154

said, "You wouldn't dare." By now, he was literally feeling no pain.

With a swift motion, Longarm shot out his left hand and grabbed Ashton's left hand. He pulled it toward the barrel of his revolver. He had Ashton almost flat on the table, his arm outstretched. He rammed the other small finger into the muzzle. Ashton screamed and began to sob and beg.

Longarm paid the man no mind. He worked the finger carefully in until it was just up to the middle knuckle. He'd take off a little more this time. He conveyed this impression to Ashton.

Ashton was crying and half screaming. "No, no, no. You can't do this. No!"

"Then show me where the money is."

"There is none. You're mistaken. I don't counterfeit. You are wrong."

"Ashton, I'm going to count to three, and I count by twos, and then you are going to lose this finger." He pulled the hammer of his revolver back. It made that deadly *clitch-clatch* sound. He was careful, however, to keep his finger away from the trigger. He really did not want to shoot off part of Ashton's other finger. One could have been an accident. Two would have been a little harder to explain.

At that instant, the door opened and Lei Chang came in, bowing and nodding his head as he came. He said, "Very sorry . . . very sorry, mister. Me, Lei Chang, me catch where money is. You want me to catch you where monies are?"

The howl that came from Vernon Ashton was enough to convince Longarm that Lei Chang really knew where the counterfeiting operation was located. He said, over Ashton's howling, "Yes, Lei Chang, I would greatly appreciate it if you'd show me where I can catchey monies. Very interested in catchey monies. Make my boss feel much better if I catchey monies. You show?''

Vernon Ashton yelled, "No, you silly Chink! No, damn it!''

Longarm suddenly got up, pulling a bandana out of his pocket, and shoved it into the open mouth of Vernon Ashton. He turned to Lei Chang, whose eyes were still riveted to the revolver lying on the table with Vernon Ashton's finger in it. Longarm said, "Very good for your boss, you showing me where to catch monies. You savvy?''

Lei Chang backed out of the room, bowing and nodding. He said, "Yes, sir. Very good. Lei Chang show place where monies is.''

Longarm said, "I'll be right with you.''

He turned, sat down at the table, and carefully worked Ashton's finger out of the muzzle of his revolver. He said, "Now, this doesn't mean that we're through shooting your fingers off. If Lei Chang is leading me on a wild-goose chase, we're going to come right back up here and do this all over again. Only this time, I ain't going to be so slow about waiting for you to answer. Do you understand?''

Ashton looked at him with vicious hatred in his eyes. He couldn't speak with the bandana shoved in his mouth, and he was afraid to reach up with his free hand and remove it. Finally, Longarm reached out and jerked the handkerchief out of his mouth, and then shoved it back in his pocket. He said, "Do you understand me, Ashton? Don't try and stop Lei Chang from showing me. I'll tell you the truth, it's for your own good. I have no plans to do anything but to make you hurt until you show me what I want to see. Understand?''

Ashton said, coldly and lowly, "You go to Hell, you sonofabitch.''

"My, my, my. I'm surprised your momma taught you to talk like that." Longarm stood up, picking up his revolver as he did. Holding it in his right hand, he went around the table and picked Ashton up by the collar of his shirt. He marched him toward the door leading out of the office. Lei Chang was backing up, preceding them while he bobbed and bowed.

The little man said, "You see by and by. You see boss makey monies. Lei Chang show in kitchen."

He led them into the library, into the big hall, into the dining room, and then through the swinging door into the kitchen. Longarm kept hold of Ashton by the collar, using his left hand. He had the revolver in his right hand, but he didn't have it pointed in any one particular place. Ashton was mumbling and cursing, and Longarm reminded him that Lei Chang was maybe doing him the biggest favor he had ever had in his life.

Longarm said, "Maybe you like pain. I don't know, but I'll tell you the truth. You are going to break before you die. You'd have shown me. If Lei Chang is showing me, he's doing you a big favor."

"That dirty heathen sonofabitch. I ought to kill him. He's been with me too many years. He's crazy."

"Let's just see if he's crazy. Maybe you're the crazy one."

Now, they were in the kitchen. It was dark, and Lei Chang lit a lantern, and then another, so that the shadows danced away from the corners.

The little man said, "I show you money." He walked across the room to an ordinary-looking door that could have been a pantry, and opened it. Ashton gave a muffled cry. Longarm walked over and looked behind the door. There seemed to be nothing there. He gave Lei Chang a questioning look. "What is this?" It was just a small room that, indeed, could have been a pantry if it had shelves.

The little man said, "You watch. Watch this." He pushed on one of the walls, and it swung away like a door and turned into a set of stairs going down into the cellar. Lei Chang was very excited. He was nodding and giggling and pointing. He said, "You see, in cellar. Catch money in cellar."

Longarm said, "Well, I'll be damned. It is. You two go ahead." He pushed the Chinese man down first, and then guided Ashton on his way down the steps.

The counterfeiter was cursing and flailing around with his free hand. Halfway down, he stopped, turned around, and looked up at Longarm, saying, "My damned hand hurts, you sonofabitch. You shot my finger off."

Longarm gave the man a shove. "Go on down there, Ashton. Let's see what we've got."

Ashton said to the Chinese man, "You damn Chink. I'm going to kill you for this."

"I don't think you're going to kill anyone, Ashton," Longarm said. "Let's just see what we have down here. Lei Chang, strike a light. Make it light in here."

The little man was already at the bottom of the cellar. He bobbed his head, and the next thing Longarm knew, two lamps had been lit. The room came into clear view. It was not an unusual-looking room, except that it was composed of concrete walls and a concrete floor. On one side of the room was an ordinary-looking printing press. Longarm walked over to it, and he could see the remains of where something about the size of eight United States currency bills had been printed at each revolution of the machinery. He didn't know much about it, but he knew that the plates or the things that had made the impression were not on the machine. Over in the corner, he could see a wooden box. Inside was what appeared to be bluish-green paper. He went over and touched the paper. It felt very much like money.

He turned and looked at Ashton. "So you weren't in the counterfeiting business, huh? What do you reckon this is?"

Ashton gave him a sullen look. "Damn it, my hand is hurting. You have to do something about my hand."

"I don't have to do a damned thing about your hand. What I have to do is have those engraved plates."

Ashton stared at him. "I just wouldn't know where they are."

Longarm said, "You'd better go to thinking very hard where they are."

He turned and looked at the Chinese man. He said, "Lei Chang, where do the boss keep big important piece of steel?"

The man nodded his head vigorously. "Oh, yes. Me catch. Very important for paper. Very important for monies. Yes, me catch."

"Where the hell are they?"

Before the Chinese man could answer, Ashton said, "Look here, whatever your name is, my hand is killing me. It's throbbing. You aren't getting any more cooperation out of me until I get some more laudanum and brandy. I need something to kill this pain."

The Chinese man said, "In safe, Boss. Very good shiny money-make stuff in safe."

Ashton fixed him with a look. He said, "You yellow sonofabitch. I'm going to chop your head off."

Longarm said, "Where is the safe, Ashton? Show me where it is."

Ashton glared at him. "It won't do you any good. You

159

can't open it, and I'm not going to until you get me some relief."

"Just show me where the damned safe is."

But instead of answering, the Chinese man came shuffling forward and went over to the far corner, almost underneath the stairs. He pulled back a cabinet door. There, set in concrete, was the steel front of a heavy-duty safe. It was not the sort of safekeeping device that you were going to blow open with a stick or two of dynamite. You'd have to blow up damned near the whole house to get the door of that safe open.

Longarm said, "Ashton, that's a combination lock. I want you to go over there and open it." He pulled out his revolver and cocked it. "If you don't, I'm going to start shooting toes off. It'll make a mess out of those fine shoes you are wearing there. I ain't seen a man on this big a ranch wearing those kind of shoes in my life. That's enough to make me shoot those toes off of you as it is."

Ashton's lip trembled, but he still said, "No, no, no. I won't open. Not unless you get me some laudanum right now. I'm telling you, the pain is so bad, I near can't bear it. I have to have some help."

Longarm thought a moment. You can't very well hurt a man who is already hurting to the extreme. He turned to the Chinese man. "Lei Chang, catch laudanum and brandy for boss. Bring catch down here. Chop, chop."

Lei Chang nodded. "Very good. Lei Chang catch and bring down here."

At that, the Chinese man set off up the stairs with his stiff-kneed trot. Longarm looked at Ashton and said, "I don't know why you want to give yourself such a hard time about this, because you are going to give in, one way or another. If I have to keep on hurting you, I'm perfectly willing to do that. I can prove right now that you are a counterfeiter with that press over there and that paper. But I want those plates out of circulation. I want that to be the little trophy I carry back to my office to show that I could do a job that I wasn't supposed to do.''

''Then what the hell are you doing here if this ain't your job?''

''Beats the hell out of me,'' Longarm said coolly. ''I guess because the Treasury Department had better sense than to come up against forty gunmen.''

''But you didn't?''

''It looks like apparently I didn't.''

''Well, if you hadn't cannonaded us with rocks and hadn't used enough dynamite on us to have dug a mine, you'd have never gotten on this property. Those men weren't afraid of a dozen devils with guns, but those explosions in the middle of the night worked on their nerves. You're to be congratulated, Deputy Marshal.''

Longarm said, ''Let's just you and me step over here and take a closer look at this safe.''

He shifted his revolver to his left hand, took Ashton by the arm, and guided him to the area right in front of the safe next to the stairs. The safe was about three feet high and four feet wide. It had a big combination lock right in the middle. Longarm said, ''You'd better start remembering that combination, Ashton, because you're going to need it in just a few minutes. When Lei Chang brings you that laudanum and it kills the pain, you are going to think you are out of the woods and that you ain't got nothing to worry about. But all I'm going to do is make you hurt all over again. This time, I'll put some hurt on you that nothing will help.''

He squatted down and brought his eyes to the level of

the dial of the safe. He noticed that it was made by the Mosler Company, which was famous for its secure safes. Many a bank robber had been frustrated trying to get inside one with a clerk who wouldn't open it. But Longarm had a clerk who was going to open it or who was going to get shot to pieces.

As he studied the safe, he became aware that somebody had come down the stairs. He didn't glance up, knowing it was Lei Chang. But then, he heard a curious hurrying sound. It came, again. It was an unusual sound that made the hair rise on the back of his neck. He took a quick glance to his right, and was shocked to see the little man charging straight toward him with a huge sword uplifted over his head in both hands.

Longarm had no time to pause, no time to think. All he could do with his revolver in his left hand was fire across his chest. The bullet hit the little man high on the shoulder, but stopped him and spun him around. Longarm rapidly cocked the pistol and fired again, this time hitting the Chinese man in the side. He went down in a heap, the big sword clattering against the hard concrete floor.

It was a second before Longarm's ears could clear from the loud blast in the concrete room. He slowly rose and looked at the shriveled figure of the little Chinese man. He glanced up at Ashton. "Did you know he was going to do that?"

Ashton gave him a cold look. "I had hopes that he would."

"He was going to go up against a heavy-caliber revolver with nothing more than a sword?"

"You have no idea what he could do with that sword. If you had been a half second later, you'd have probably been twins."

Chapter 10

Lei Chang had left the brandy and the laudanum on the landing at the top of the stairs. Longarm went up and fetched it, and then poured Ashton a glass of half-and-half. The counterfeiter wolfed it down, and then asked for more brandy. Longarm was only too happy to help him.

After Ashton had finished drinking, Longarm said, "Now, in a minute or two, you are not going to be hurting, and that's when you're going to decide that you won't open this safe. I'm not going to tell you what is going to happen then. I'm going to let you figure it out yourself."

Vernon Ashton drew himself up to his full height, which brought him only to Longarm's shoulders. He said, "You have no right to make me open that safe. You have no warrant to be in this house. You are overreaching your authority, and I demand that you leave right now."

Longarm stared at him in disbelief. "Are you drunk or what? You must not have noticed that I shot your finger off and that I really don't much care what I do to you." He stared a moment longer at Ashton. "I don't understand you, mister." He turned and looked at where the Chinese man lay like a little heap of rags. "There is that Chinese fellow. Got himself killed for you. There are three or four others upstairs that are dead on account of you. There's your foreman, Early. He's out there dead on account of you. There are how many others who are dead on account of you. Who the hell do you think you are? You know, I'm near about to get sick of you. Do you understand me?''

Ashton said, ''You can't tell me—''

He got no further. Longarm suddenly said, ''Oh, hell. I'm sick of this.'' He shoved his revolver in his holster and reached out and grabbed Ashton by his injured hand. With a twist of his wrist, he shoved the man's arm up behind him, high enough that Ashton had to go up on tiptoe to keep something from cracking. He got his face down next to Ashton's ear. ''Now, you feel that? You're screaming a little bit already. A little more, and I'll lift you off the floor with this arm. You'll either come off the floor or something is going to break, or you can open that safe. Now, you can make up your mind which it's going to be. I'm tired of fooling with you. I'll break you up little by little.''

Longarm curled his left arm around Ashton's neck, pulling his head back. With his other arm, he forced Ashton's right arm up between his shoulder blades. It was as if he was trying to make Ashton touch the back of his head with the back of his hand. Ashton was emitting a loud scream that grew in intensity and tenor with every passing instant. Longarm was wasting no time. With his head down and his ear next to Ashton's shoulders, he could hear creaking and crackling sounds. He figured the man's shoulder or elbow or something would go any second.

Then Ashton yelled out, ''All right! All right!''

Longarm eased off the slightest bit. He said, ''What?''

Ashton's voice was still high-pitched and full of a

scream. He said, "All right! I'll open the damned safe. Don't hurt me anymore."

Longarm slowly let the arm down to about halfway. He said, "I'm going to give you a chance. But if you don't open that safe immediately, if this is some method of stalling and thinking that you can get it to stop hurting for a little while, it ain't going to work. If you don't open that safe, I'm going to grab you right back up and jam this arm of yours into the back of your head. I'm going to break it clean in two. Do you understand?"

Ashton panted and made whimpering sounds.

"I said, do you understand?"

Finally, Ashton said, "Yes, yes. I understand. I'll open the safe."

Longarm shoved the man down to his knees in front of the big heavy strongbox. He said, "Then get busy."

For a moment, Ashton sagged on his knees and worked his right arm, trying to ease the pain.

Longarm said, "Hurry up."

Ashton said, "It hurts so badly, it's going to take me a second."

Longarm pulled out his revolver and tapped the man on his silver-streaked hair. He said, "Get busy, damn it."

Ashton raised his right hand up with the bandaged little finger and awkwardly twisted the knob of the safe, first to the left and then to the right. Finally, he grasped the handle of the iron door and shoved it downward. There was a distinct click and the door opened half an inch. Longarm unceremoniously shoved Ashton aside and leaned down, took hold of the handle, and pulled the heavy door open. Inside was a wooden box about the size of a small loaf of bread.

Longarm said, "Is that it?"

Ashton nodded. "Yeah. There's another set in the back of the safe, but they are the backups. They are nearly worn out, so we stopped using them."

Longarm squatted down and picked up the box. It was surprisingly heavy. He pulled it out of the safe and set it on the floor in front of him. He opened the lid. Inside were two shiny steel plates about seven or eight inches long and about four inches wide. He took one out and looked at it. It was beautifully and exquisitely engraved. It was clear even to his untrained eye that it was the front part of a twenty-dollar bill. He took out another plate, and saw that it was the reverse, the back of the bill. He put both of the plates back in the box and carefully closed it.

He stood up. "You saved yourself a lot of pain, Mr. Ashton. Now, I'm going to leave you alone for a little while."

Panic suddenly came on Ashton's face. He said, "You are not going to leave me down here? Not with that over there!" He pointed to where Lei Chang lay dead.

Longarm said, "Look, you've got plenty of brandy and plenty of laudanum for pain. It ought to make any bad memories you've got go away. I'm not going to be gone long. I see there's a jug of water over in the corner. You'll be all right. It ain't near time for breakfast yet."

He turned and went up the stairs that led into the pantry-like room just off the kitchen. When he got in the room, he pulled on a rope and the stairs rose up, folding so that now they looked like a section of a wooden wall. He pulled it all the way shut and the rope slipped through, so that there was no sign of a stair unless you knew where to look.

He stepped out of the room, shut the door, and locked it with the key that was there. Ashton had put up quite a howl when he had left, but Longarm wasn't too concerned about that. He wanted one more look around, and he wanted to check on the man he'd left with the wound in the thigh. He doubted if the damned fool had used the tourniquet correctly. More than likely, he had bled to death by now. But Longarm owed him at least a look. He was, when all was said and done, a United States deputy marshal, even if he did have to deal with such cur dogs as Vernon Ashton. There had been a lot of people killed over that little wooden box that he was carrying under his arm.

Inside the safe he had noticed stacks of twenty-dollar bills. He hadn't noticed if they were real or not, but he had noticed a box that was full of the same things. He didn't know too many people that kept boxes of twenty-dollar bills sitting around in their cellar. He was quite sure he was looking at a box of counterfeit twenty-dollar bills.

But that was of no concern to him. His job was nearly over. He would take a quick look upstairs at the man with the tourniquet, and unless there was a reason for him to stay any longer, he'd get on his horse and head back to town, and wrap things up and catch the first train he could back to Denver.

He mounted the stairs of the curving stairway, and went up to the second floor into the long wide hall. He walked down it, his boots sidling on the carpet, his spurs not even making a sound. He wondered where the girl had gone. He wondered where her matron or nurse or guard or chaperone—whatever they call them in Mexico or Spain or wherever she was from—was. He hadn't seen her. He walked past all the closed doors and down to the end.

He went through the short hall, and then opened the door into the storage room where the young gunman lay on the floor. One look told Longarm he was too late. The young man had slid down until he was flat on the floor. His hands had come loose from the stick he had wound the tourniquet with, and Longarm could tell that a great deal of blood had flowed. He didn't know if the young man had grown too weak to keep the pressure, or if he had kept it on too long and cut off the circulation and his leg had gone to sleep and then *he* had gone to sleep. Anyway, he was dead, sleeping forever.

Longarm shifted the box over under his left arm, and then turned and went out of the room, closing the door behind him. He still had one revolver in his waistband in the small of his back and one revolver in his holster. His rifle was downstairs, just off the kitchen by the door to the back, where he had killed the man with the shotgun. Longarm walked slowly down the hall, alert. In such a place, he was never certain just how many of them were there. But he felt quite safe now that he had Vernon Ashton under lock and key. A good many of them were dangerous men, but none of them were really dangerous without Ashton's money to buy their evil deeds and their evil ways. If there was anyone dangerous on the whole place, he was now in the cellar with the dead Lei Chang.

Longarm was about to let his mind start to think about the ride back to town when the door to the right suddenly opened. It was the door the girl had come out before. It was flung open so that she stood fully in the open. He could see now that she was still wearing the same housedress or nightgown, whichever way you wanted to look at it, but this time, she hadn't bothered with any buttons. Her breasts were clearly revealed, straight and erect, as was the shiny patch of fur that grew on the soft mound where her legs met.

Longarm stopped. He didn't know what to do. She was no more than six feet away from him. By rights, he should walk on by her, get on his horse, and ride on back into town and finish the job. But then, she was a job that he had twice never quite been able to finish.

He took a step toward her. Her lips parted and she stepped backward. He took another step, and she kept walking back. Soon, he was inside the door, and she had backed until the back of her legs had met the bed in the opulent room. She sat down, her dress flaring out all around her.

He stopped within two feet of her and stood staring down at her, feeling his groin get thick and his jeans get too small and that copper taste come in his mouth. There was a small table near the head of the bed. He reached over and set the box of engraved plates on it. His eyes came back to her. She was sitting there, her head back and her mouth slightly open. She ran her tongue around her lips. Her eyes were black and fiery. She leaned back further on the bed so that he could see where the black silken hairs ran into the pink flesh. Longarm took another step toward her. She suddenly raised up and began frantically trying to undo his gun belt. He took her hands away quickly. He didn't want her to know about the derringer that was concealed in the buckle. Instead, he undid the belt himself and let it fall to the floor.

He reached behind himself and pulled the other revolver out of his waistband. She attacked the belt that held up his pants with fierce energy and flying fingers. In a moment, he was standing open with his member erect. She buried her head, sinking him deep into her mouth. Longarm shivered and clutched her to him. He pitched the revolver up toward the head of the bed near the pillow. He was pushing her back, his pants down around his ankles.

She worked herself up on the bed until her head was up at the pillows. She opened her legs wide to receive him.

With her soft hand, she cleverly guided him inside her. Then her legs were around his hips, and she was pulling him back and forth with a motion that was almost more than he could stand. Inside, she was so hot that he could feel the heat of her through his shirt. She was kissing him with fevered kisses with a wide-open mouth and a darting tongue. He clutched her to him, letting her do the work, only pumping in response to her thrusts. He could feel himself going up and up and up until there was a sudden crescendo. It was like the explosion of the dynamite, only it seemed bigger and louder and made more noise. It was as if the mountains all around were being leveled.

Longarm went up and up to the very top, and then tumbled down as they exploded, going boom and boom and boom, until finally there were no more mountains and no more explosions. He sagged limply on her. He could feel her wet kisses on his face. He could feel her hands clawing at his back. She was saying in his ear, "More! More!"

He gasped out when he could, "Honey, you're going to have to give me a minute or two. I'm not as young as I used to be."

"Please, you don't let me stay like this. Please."

She hunched up against him, trying to work him and bring vigor back to his member. He said, "Honey, you can't whip a dead horse."

It was in that instant that he became aware of movement to the left. He turned his face quickly, half expecting to see the girl's maid or chaperone.

It was neither. It was Finley.

Longarm was so surprised, he said, "What the hell?"

Finley was holding a gun in his hand. He was just inside the door. He said, "Well, howdy, Mr. Long. You look like you're having a good time."

Longarm said, "What the hell are you doing here?"

The man just grinned. "Well, she's just gave you a really good fucking. I'm about to give you another." He reached into his pocket and pulled out a little piece of leather. Attached to it was a badge. "This may come as a surprise to you, U.S. Deputy Marshal Custis Long. But I'm a United States Treasury agent and I'm taking charge of this case."

Longarm was slowly pulling out of the girl. He was conscious that he was standing in front of another man who had a gun in his hand and his pants were down. He glanced casually up along the side of the bed that was hidden from Finley's view by the girl's body. His second gun was just by her side. As he started to raise up a little, he flipped the cover over the gun so that it couldn't be seen from any angle.

His mind was in a whirl. All of a sudden the man he had thought was a stockman and a poker player and a fairly friendly fellow turned out to be a Treasury agent, one that was intent on having things his own way.

Longarm said slowly, "All right. So you're a Treasury agent. What does that mean, you're taking over the case? Whatever a case is. I've had a case of whiskey and I've had a case of the clap, but I don't know what this case is."

Finley pushed his hat up a little bit with his left hand and gave his revolver a circular motion with his right. He said, "It means that this is all mine. It means that we are going to pretend that you never existed."

"Exactly what do you mean by that?"

Finley grinned, and it was not particularly pleasing to see. He said, "Well, if your superiors had been giving you hell on account of you couldn't stop this one counterfeiter, you'd understand how I feel. If you were in my position and you were able to take that case yonder"—he nodded

171

at the box of steel engravings—"into headquarters and say look here what I've got. I've got the engraving plates. I've got the paper. I've got the specimens they call the counterfeit stuff. I've got the man who done it."

"So you plan to go in and tell them that you did it all on your own. Is that it?"

Finley smiled again. His teeth were a little yellow, Longarm noticed for the first time. Finley said, "Well, don't you think it would sound a little better if it sounded like I did it all on my own. Look at all the opposition I had at this place. Look at all the opposition I've overcome. Look at the hell of a job I did. I must have killed about fifteen or twenty of these sonofabitches. I killed Early, who was wanted all over the country, and now I have the boss man, Vernon Ashton, locked up in the cellar. Hell, it looks to me like I've done a good job. Looks like I busted up the whole ring."

Longarm had come to his knees and was pulling up his pants, buttoning the buttons one at a time. His mind was racing. He said, "I guess I'm kind of in the way for you to be able to tell a story like that. Is that what you're saying?"

"Well, Mr. Long, I'm sure you can see the right of it. Or should I say, Deputy Long. I mean, that's going to make me a big man in the Treasury Department, doing a deal like this. This man's been giving us fits for several years. My boss has been giving me fits for several years. Now, here you are. You've done a fine job. I've admired every step you've taken."

Longarm said, "You know, I've always had the sensation that somebody was watching me. That somebody was looking over my shoulder. I could never really see them, but I felt them."

Finley chuckled. "Well, your feelings were right. I'm real good at becoming invisible when I need to. Yes, sir. I've watched every step you took. I knew when you left the hotel with that first load of dynamite. I saw you go up that first hill and blow that first load of rocks down on them. I thought then that you were one smart fellow. You knew what you were doing. You were going to make them so scared that they're going to come out. Then you were going to go in. You weren't going in and go up against those forty-to-one odds. No, sir. You had brains. So, I just naturally let you lead on. Tonight, I was right behind you. I took every step for you. In fact, I finished off one job for you. There was a young fellow down the hall that had a tourniquet on. That was a damn fool thing to do. What the hell did you want to leave a witness like him around for? I undid that tourniquet and let him bleed to death. That was a nice thing, don't you think?"

Longarm sat back slowly on the edge of the bed. He looked at Finley and shook his head slowly. "Finley, you're a rare sonofabitch. You mean to tell me that you're going to take credit for this whole thing? What about me?"

"You? Can't you figure that out? Anyone that fools around with dynamite as much as you've been fooling around with it—and there are plenty of records about how much dynamite you've bought at that store—well, sooner or later, they're likely to blow themselves to pieces. I'd reckon that's what happened to you."

"So, you're going to make it seem like I didn't even exist?"

"Well, what would you do in my place?"

Longarm said, "I don't know. I've never been in the place of a low-down no-good sonofabitch before." He leaned forward, putting his weight on his right hand, letting

173

it slip under the covers and grasp the butt of his revolver. He did it under the guise of inching one foot off the bed and toward the floor. "You don't mind if I get up from here, do you?"

Finley shook his head. "No. As a matter of fact, I'm going to need you to come on and go with me. We're going to ride off a ways, just me and you."

"Are both of us coming back?"

Finley chuckled. "Well, I wouldn't know about that."

For the first time, Longarm noticed the girl. Her eyes were wide with fright. She probably didn't know what was happening, but she knew that something very dangerous was taking place. She couldn't know whether or not she would be caught in the cross fire. Longarm knew that he damned sure couldn't tell her.

He went on easing himself off the bed, dragging his right hand under the protection of the covers that had been thrown back to receive the body of the girl as she lay on her back. Out of his left eye, because he didn't want Finley to think he was watching him too close, Longarm could see that Finley was glancing from time to time at the case on the table.

Longarm said, "You might want to check those plates. They might be the wrong ones. There's another set downstairs."

"You don't say? Is that a fact?"

"Yes, that's a fact."

Finley said, "Well, I reckon I ought to. . . ." He took a step toward the table, turning himself slightly sideways to Longarm. It took the aim of his gun a few degrees off dead center. In that instant, Longarm reacted. He came out from under the covers with the revolver, letting his foot hit the floor. He fell sideways. He fired as he was about halfway to the floor. He saw the bullet hit Finley in the side of the chest and saw the man stagger sideways. Finley fired his gun, but it was aimed toward the ceiling. White dust came down.

As Longarm hit the floor, he cocked his revolver and fired again, this time hitting Finley in the throat.

The last bullet did it. Finley slammed into the wall, and then slid slowly down until he was sitting on the floor. He was dead, but he just hadn't fallen over. His lifeless fingers still held the gun. Blood was beginning to seep from the two holes.

Longarm sat up slowly. The room was filled with the booming of the shots and the acrid smell of gunpowder. He said, ''Well, Longarm, now you've really done it. Now you've killed yourself a Treasury agent. If they weren't mad enough at you before, they are going to be mad as hell now.''

He looked over at the girl. She was staring at him with wide eyes. But then slowly her lips parted and she let her tongue run out around her lips. She said, ''Softly, please. Now. Please.''

Longarm got quickly to his feet and picked up his gun belt. He said, ''Are you crazy? Every time I fuck you, something bad happens. Somebody gets shot. This place is full of bad stuff. They've got counterfeit money, counterfeit women and now, counterfeit Treasury agents. Hell, I can't keep up with it. I've got to get to Denver to where it's real. How in the hell I'm going to explain all this, I don't know. I don't have the slightest idea. Maybe Billy Vail is the only man alive that I know who will believe me. Doesn't mean he'll take my side, but he will believe me.''

He looked at the girl again. ''Yeah, I guess that's what I'll call you. The counterfeit woman in the counterfeit house with the counterfeit money and the counterfeit Treasury agent. All in all, this has been a counterfeit case. Can you say that word? It's a new one I've learned. . . . counterfeit case.''

The girl just looked at him in bewilderment. Longarm said, ''Don't feel bad. I don't understand it either.''

All there was left to do was go downstairs, fetch Ashton out of the cellar, and head for town, taking the engraved plates and some of the paper and some of the specimens, as Finley had called them, and then head for Denver.

He started out the door, and then looked down at the dead man. The badge that Finley had shown him was peeking out of his shirt pocket. Longarm reached down and plucked it out to have a closer look. Sure enough, it was a real Treasury agent's badge. ''Damn!'' Longarm said as he dropped it back in the man's lap. ''The one damned thing in this whole counterfeit operation that had to turn out to be real, he had to be a real Treasury agent. Boy, Billy Vail is going to give me some hell about this.''

He looked around at the girl. He said, ''Well, *adios. Buenas suerte*.''

She said, leaning toward him, ''Please, once more.''

''You really are crazy. I've got to get on my way. I've got a lot of chickens to kill.'' He took the box under his arm and started down the hall. The job was finished, and he wasn't sure that he wasn't also. Killing Treasury agents, even with a damned good cause, was probably going to be looked on sort of dimly. He had no earthly idea of what he was in for.

Chapter 11

Longarm had been back in Denver for about a week. He was sitting on the bed in the boardinghouse, smoking cigarillos and drinking Maryland whiskey. He stared out the window. He didn't believe he'd ever had any more trouble getting out of a mess in all of his life. Just getting the whole thing explained to the sheriff in Silverton had been a job of work in itself.

After that, getting enough people to go out and help him clean up the bodies on the Ashton place had been another headache. The townspeople, when they discovered that he had shut Ashton down, had come damned close to lynching him. He had shoved Ashton into the sheriff's jail, but the first night, it was a near guess as to who was going to end up there, him or Vernon Ashton. Only the good efforts of the sheriff had prevented a riot. The people hadn't given a damn if he was a United States deputy marshal or not. All they knew was that he had cut off their cash. It was only when things settled down a little bit that some of them began to realize that the money they had taken in and had been passing along wasn't real money after all. By that time, other Treasury agents had come in—regular Treasury agents, ones not anxious to take all the credit. They had spread out through the town and collected what they still called specimens.

That was when the town had turned against Ashton. Take a specimen twenty-dollar bill away from a storekeeper, and his attitude will take a swift turn in a hurry. They didn't care the twenty-dollar bills were specimens and were going to be used in a case against Ashton. All they knew was that where there had been a twenty-dollar bill, there was nothing now.

Of course, not many of the counterfeit bills had found their way to Silverton, and when they had, it had been quite by accident. Ashton was no fool. He wasn't going to foul his own nest. Most of his bogus money had been sent off to the East and up into Yankee land, where there would be no connection with his base of operations. But nevertheless, there were some twenties some of the men had apparently stolen and used in town. So, when the townspeople had discovered what line of work Ashton was in, their opinions had done a somersault, and Ashton's reputation had come up snake eyes.

In the end, Longarm had gotten it all cleaned up. He'd turned over Ashton, the plates, the paper that was used in the manufacture of the bogus money, the counterfeit printing press, and the body of Finley. The agents had had very little comment about what had transpired between him and Finley. That, he knew, would be played out back in Denver between himself and Billy Vail.

To his great surprise, Billy Vail had understood. In fact, he'd even known about Finley. He'd said, ''Finley is just someone gone wrong in office, Custis. It happens in our service, it happens in the Treasury service, hell, it happens in all government services. The man just went wrong and let his ambition get ahead of him. He wanted to settle that case. It had come to his ears that you were on it and that you had a better chance than most to crack that case open. So, he was going to let you do the work and he was going to take the credit. Finley already had a reputation for being a little too handy with a gun, and the Treasury Department doesn't much care for that kind. I told them the facts of what happened. They are disposed as to believe it. In fact, I have demanded an apology for one of their officers interfering with one of mine in his line of duty. I believe we are going to get it. So, you got out of another one, you scoundrel. Anyway, it sounds like you did a pretty good job. I don't know how you keep getting so lucky, but I guess you do.''

Longarm yawned and stretched. He was wearing nothing but a pair of Levi's. He had just had a bath down the hall, and he was fresh and clean and feeling good. It was coming on toward dark and in a little while, his lady friend who ran the dress shop was going to stop by his room, and they were going to have a reunion before they went to eat dinner. He was looking forward to that reunion with Pauline. He had missed her dearly on that long trip across the mountains, but now, he figured he could make up for lost time in just a little while. There sure as hell wasn't anything counterfeit about Pauline.

Watch for

LONGARM AND THE RED-LIGHT LADIES

242nd novel in the exciting LONGARM series
from Jove

Coming in February!